LUCK OF THE DRAW

As Skye Fargo entered the trading post, he heard the sound of cards being ruffled. The only person in the place was Curry, seated at a table playing solitaire.

Skye halted in front of the table. "Your card-playing days are over."

"I've been expecting you," the gunman said, unruffled. "Figured it would be you and me eventually."

"Stand up," Skye said.

Curry made no move to comply. He deposited a red queen on a black king. "What's your hurry to die, Trailsman?"

In this part of the West, Curry was king of the killers. And in the game they were playing, the only way to top a king was to come up with bullets. . . .

THE
TRAILSMAN
128

SNAKE
RIVER
BUTCHER

by

Jon Sharpe

SIGNET
Published by the Penguin Group
Penguin Books USA Inc., 375 Hudson Street,
New York, New York 10014, U.S.A.
Penguin Books Ltd, 27 Wrights Lane,
London W8 5TZ, England
Penguin Books Australia Ltd, Ringwood,
Victoria, Australia
Penguin Books Canada Ltd, 10 Alcorn Avenue,
Toronto, Ontario, M4V 3B2
Penguin Books (N.Z.) Ltd, 182-190 Wairau Road,
Auckland 10, New Zealand

Penguin Books Ltd, Registered Offices:
Harmondsworth, Middlesex, England

First published by Signet,
an imprint of New American Library,
a division of Penguin Books USA Inc.

First Printing, August, 1992
10 9 8 7 6 5 4 3 2 1

The first chapter of this book previously appeared in *Nevada Warpath*, the one hundred twenty-seventh volume in this series.

 REGISTERED TRADEMARK—MARCA REGISTRADA

Printed in the United States of America

The Trailsman

Beginnings . . . they bend the tree and they mark the man. Skye Fargo was born when he was eighteen. Terror was his midwife, vengeance his first cry. Killing spawned Skye Fargo, ruthless, cold-blooded murder. Out of the acrid smoke of gunpowder still hanging in the air, he rose, cried out a promise never forgotten.

The Trailsman they began to call him all across the West: searcher, scout, hunter, the man who could see where others only looked, his skills for hire but not his soul, the man who lived each day to the fullest, yet trailed each tomorrow. Skye Fargo, the Trailsman, the seeker who could take the wildness of a land and the wanting of a woman and make them his own.

1859, the Snake River region,
where those who traveled the Oregon Trail
did so at their own risk . . .

1

The big man astride the splendid pinto stallion reined up abruptly as he topped a rise and saw the five men camped below on the bank of the Snake River. A thin column of smoke wafted skyward from their camp fire, and the breeze carried the delicious aroma of brewing coffee to his sensitive nostrils. His stomach growled, reminding him that he had not had a decent cup of coffee in days. Although he had rationed his supply, he had run out on the long trail from Denver to the remote, rugged Snake River country.

Ordinarily Skye Fargo kept to himself. But he was new to the area and had heard rumors of Indian trouble. It might be wise to learn what he could before he ventured further on his quest, and with that in mind he touched his spurs to the Ovaro's muscular flanks and rode directly toward the camp.

One of the men spotted him right away and said something to the rest that brought all of them to their feet, rifles in hand. They were a grubby lot, wearing soiled flannel shirts, faded, patched trousers, and hats that had seen better days ages ago.

As Skye neared the camp his every instinct told him he had made a mistake. He saw expressions of blatant envy on the faces of several of the bunch as they admired his stallion and his gear, and he noticed the tallest of the lot whisper to the others and immediately a burly character started to edge off to the right while another man did likewise on the left. They were so obvious he almost laughed. Instead he rested his right hand on his thigh within inches of his Colt.

"Howdy, stranger," the tall one greeted him with a

generous smile that revealed several of his front teeth were missing.

Fargo drew rein ten feet away and simply nodded. He stared at the speaker but kept track of the pair trying not so cleverly to outflank him.

"Light and sit a while," the tall man said, motioning at the battered coffeepot beside the crackling flames. "We have plenty of coffee if you're thirsty."

"Another time," Fargo said pleasantly, letting them think they had him duped so they would be all the more shocked when he demonstrated otherwise.

The tall one advanced a stride, the barrel of his rifle slowly inching higher. "What can we do for you then?"

"Back in Denver there was talk of Indian trouble in this neck of the woods. Have you had any problem?"

"Us?" the tall one said, and most of them snickered as if at a joke. "Can't say as we have. There were some Mormons east of here a ways who got run off a while back. A few were killed and scalped, as I recollect." He smirked. "But they were just no-account Mormons."

"Too bad it wasn't you and your outfit," Fargo said.

The tall man blinked, perhaps not believing he had heard correctly, and then he realized he had and began to elevate the rifle, his finger sliding over the trigger.

Skye Fargo was in no mood to go easy on the cutthroats. He had been riding hard for more days than he cared to remember and he was tired and sore and hungry. His right hand was a blur as the Colt flashed up and out, and his first shot tore into the tall man's throat. His second shot, so closely spaced the twin blasts were one sound, ripped into the man's chest and staggered him. The tall man let go of his rifle, spun, and toppled.

Fargo was already in motion, twisting to send a slug into the forehead of the skinny sidewinder on the right who was trying to bring his rifle to bear. Then he shifted again, covering the remaining three, all of whom froze as if abruptly encased in ice. "Any more of you anxious to meet your Maker?" he asked calmly, and cocked the Colt to accent his meaning.

"Don't shoot, mister!" blurted a man sporting a walrus mustache. He tossed his rifle to the ground. "Please don't shoot!"

The other two followed his example and in moments

all three were clawing for the clouds without having been ordered to do so.

"I was hoping you'd make a fight of it," Fargo said and gestured with the Colt to indicate they should back up past the fire. "Unload your hardware," he directed, and once they had gingerly discarded their pistols he swung down, being careful to keep his six-shooter on them the whole time, then stepped to the fire. "This coffee sure does smell good," he commented, bending to lift the pot. The bottom was hot but the top rim only warm. He tilted the narrow spout and took a sip, then smacked his lips. "Who made this?"

Walrus pointed at the tall man, lying prone in a spreading puddle of blood. "Harry did."

"He wasn't much of a robber, but he had a knack for making a fine brew," Skye quipped and swallowed some more.

"What do you aim to do with us?" Walrus inquired nervously.

"I should shoot you."

"No!" exclaimed the bearded man on the left. "I have a wife and kids. You can't!"

Slowly, deliberately, Fargo pointed the Colt at him and the man took a step to the rear, his lips quivering in abject fear, his legs trembling as if he had to take a leak and was desperately holding it in.

"Please!" he whined. "We never meant to harm you."

Fargo shot him. The revolver boomed and bucked in his hand, and the man reacted in the same way as would someone slammed by a sledgehammer, by flying a good three feet to crash down on his back. His features hard as granite, Fargo took a few steps forward. The other two were imitating trees.

"Oh, God!" the man on the ground wailed, clutching the neat hole in his right shoulder and writhing in torment. "You plugged me! You plugged me!"

"I can do it again if you don't shut up."

The man fell silent, gritting his teeth.

"I can't abide liars," Fargo stated gruffly. "Particularly when they were fixing to kill me and steal everything I own."

"We weren't—" the wounded man protested, then caught himself and clamped his thin lips shut.

"That's better," Fargo said, moving back around the fire. He squatted and sipped more of the refreshing coffee, his gaze roving over their shabby clothes and to their horses tethered nearby. "Strange," he said.

Walrus took the bait. "What is, mister?"

"All of you could pass for walking rags but you all own horses as fine as any I've ever seen," Fargo noted. "Why is that?"

"A good horse out in these parts can mean the difference between living and dying," Walrus replied. "You know that." He paused. "We'd rather spend our money on a fine horse any day than on new Levi's. Pants and such can't outrun Injuns."

The shifty bastard had a point, but Fargo didn't believe him for a second. Still, he couldn't prove anything and despite what these men might believe, he wasn't a cold-hearted murderer. "Were I you I would make myself scarce in this territory," he informed them. "I'll probably be wandering around for a while, and if I ever lay eyes on any of you again you'd better be able to slap leather faster than me."

"None of us are that fast," said the robber who had not uttered a word until now.

"Should help you decide what to do," Fargo said, rising so he could arch his back and stretch. "How far is it to Fort Hall?"

"About fifteen miles," Walrus answered.

Fargo glanced at the gurgling river, estimating the depth. "I'd be willing to bet none of you gents have bothered to take a bath this year, have you?"

They exchanged worried looks.

"So?" Walrus answered.

"So I figure it's time for all of you to take one," Fargo said and nodded at the waterway that some claimed flowed over a thousand miles, all the way from the Continental Divide in the northern Rockies to where it merged into the mighty Columbia River a few hundred miles shy of the Pacific Ocean. "Jump in."

"You're loco!" Walrus declared.

Fargo grinned and wagged the Colt. "Some folks might agree with you. But I figure I'm doing the next whore you sleep with a favor by sparing her nose some misery. So don't be shy. Jump right in, clothes and all."

None of them moved. The robber on the ground groaned loudly, his hand pressed tight over the bullet hole.

"I'm waiting," Fargo said.

Walrus shook his head. "No way, stranger. I'll be damned if I will."

"You'll be dead if you don't."

Scowling in disgust, the third man moved to the edge of the low bank and contemplated the shallow water flowing sluggishly past. He bent down to dip a hand in the cold water and shivered. "I'll freeze my ass off."

"It's better than lead poisoning," Fargo pointed out, enjoying himself immensely. These men had asked for trouble by stupidly trying to rob him and he intended to give them an object lesson they wouldn't soon forget. He suspected the gang had a string of robberies and perhaps killings to their credit. They probably deserved to be the guests of honor at a necktie party, but he wasn't a vigilante. He watched the wounded man stand, and together the trio stepped tentatively into the Snake. When the water swirled past their ankles they halted. "Keep on going," he directed.

Exhibiting as much enthusiasm as they would if they were being forced to wrestle a grizzly, the three robbers walked out farther. The water level rose to their knees and again they stopped.

"Not yet," Fargo told them and cracked a grin. The ploy served a twofold purpose. Not only did it humiliate them, but it would leave them in no position to try and shoot him in the back when he departed. He moved to where their discarded revolvers lay and began picking them up.

"What the hell are you doing now?" demanded the man with the mustache.

"You can't leave us defenseless!" cried the wounded one.

"I'm tempted," Fargo responded. "But even sons of bitches like you deserve a chance to protect themselves." He walked over to a dense thicket and proceeded to toss the revolvers one at a time into the heaviest tangle of growth.

"We'll remember you for this, mister," Walrus said.

"I'm shaking in my boots," Fargo said and gathered

their rifles into his arms. He strolled to the river, deposited his burden at his feet, then gripped one of the weapons by the barrel and hefted it.

"No!" Walrus shouted.

Ignoring him, Fargo swept his arm to one side, then whipped the rifle forward and released his grip. Sunlight glinted off the metal as the rifle sailed end over end and splashed down a dozen yards up river from the would-be robbers. One by one he tossed each rifle as far as he could, and when the last of the long guns lay at the bottom of the Snake, he turned his attention to his crestfallen enemies who were standing in waist-deep water. "Keep on going," he instructed them.

If looks could kill they would have shriveled him like a withering plant.

When the Snake rose to just under their arms Fargo twirled his Colt into its holster and beamed. "That should do, boys. Thanks for the entertainment." Pivoting, he went to their horses and commenced untying every animal.

"You have a name, bastard?" Walrus called out. "I want to know who to ask for."

"The handle is Skye Fargo," he informed them and heard the excited muttering that ensued. Given the tales told about him around many a campfire and in many a saloon from the Mississippi to California, he wouldn't be at all surprised if they had heard of him. Not that it mattered in the least. He paid no attention to his notoriety. His main concern during all his widespread traveling was simply staying alive.

He removed his hat and slapped it on the rump of the nearest horse. "Heeyaahhh!" he bellowed, then waved the hat wildly and jumped up and down several times. The horses wheeled and raced westward, raising a small cloud of dust in their wake, and were soon lost to view in a tract of woodland.

Feeling quite pleased with himself, Fargo walked to the Ovaro and mounted. The three men were glaring sullenly. He added insult to injury by giving a cheery wave and resumed his journey, heading in the general direction he expected to find Fort Hall. Several times he glanced back. When he had gone over a hundred yards the three men waded to shore and clambered out of the river. The one with the walrus mustache shook a fist and shouted obscenities, then all three hurried to the thicket where their six-shooters had been tossed.

Fargo wasn't worried. The range was too great for an accurate pistol shot, and those three had impressed him as being unable to hit the broad side of a steamboat with a paddle. Soon he came to the woodland and angled to the northwest. There had been few trees the last twenty miles or better and he was grateful for the shade. A last look showed one of the robbers venturing into the Snake in an attempt to retrieve the rifles.

He put the trio from his mind as of no further importance and pressed on. There was an hour or so of daylight left and he wanted to take full advantage of the time to get as close to Fort Hall as he could before night set in. He'd decided earlier to hold off entering the fort until the next morning. A good night's sleep would refresh him for the job ahead.

The Snake River area abounded with wildlife. There were birds everywhere—sparrows flitting about, a few gorgeous tanagers perched on the highest branches, nutcrackers seeking food, and an occasional woodpecker or two. Daredevil squirrels leaped from tree to tree while chipmunks scampered among the boulders.

Skye Fargo breathed deep of the pine scent and patted his stallion on the neck. This was his element. He much preferred the open wild places to the wood and brick mazes that passed for cities and towns. Not that he disliked companionship. There were scores of fallen doves scattered throughout the West who could attest to his friendliness.

He stifled a yawn and gazed to the west. He'd been in the saddle since first light, except for two brief stops to give the pinto a rest, and he welcomed the prospect of making camp. Too bad he hadn't thought to borrow some of the robbers' coffee.

The woods thinned out, and by the time the sun hung above the horizon he came to a creek flowing south toward the Snake. Erosion had worn a shallow gully that was perfect for his needs. He rode down the slight slope and reined up. There was plenty of water, shelter from the wind, and no one on the plain above would be able to see them.

Skye swung down and let the stallion drink. He stripped off his saddle, his saddlebags, and the bedroll, then moved aside while the pinto rolled to its heart's delight. Next he took a picket pin, used a rock to pound it into the ground, and tethered the Ovaro in the middle of a lush patch of grass.

The horse attended to, he took care of his own needs. Collecting enough dry wood to last through the night took twenty minutes, and twilight shrouded the landscape when he stretched out on his blankets beside the flickering fire and chewed hungrily on a piece of jerked beef. Tomorrow he planned to treat himself to a hot meal before he got down to business. And a drink or two to wash down the dust from weeks of travel wouldn't hurt either.

A myriad of stars blossomed in the heavens and Fargo lay there for almost an hour staring and pondering on how best to go about the job he had to do. Growing thirsty he rose and walked to the creek where he knelt, propped his palms on a flat rock at the water's edge, and drank heartily. Straightening, he wiped his mouth with the back of his sleeve.

The Ovaro nickered.

Fargo stood and turned. He'd ridden the stallion long enough to know the difference between an ordinary neigh and the way it whinnied when it was agitated, and right now it was agitated. A moment later he discovered why.

Slinking down the far side of the gully was one of the largest mountain lions he had ever seen.

2

Skye was surprised more than anything else. The big cats seldom bothered humans. Ordinarily they turned tail and ran at the faintest whiff of human scent. Yet there had been instances when lone travelers, trappers, and mountain men had been attacked and mauled. Most had survived, but not all.

This particular cat was interested in the Ovaro. Body held low to the ground, its tail twitching with each careful step, the tawny beast slunk toward the tethered pinto.

As much as Skye Fargo appreciated all wild things and although he never killed an animal unless it was absolutely necessary, he wasn't about to stand idly by and let his prized horse be slain and eaten. He placed his right hand on the butt of his Colt and advanced slowly, hoping his mere proximity would convince the mountain lion to flee. No such luck. The cat glanced at him, then kept on stalking the stallion.

"Persistent devil," Skye said aloud in the hope the alien sound of his voice would do the trick. Again it ignored him. "You're asking for it," he declared.

At last the mountain lion stopped and regarded him balefully.

Fargo moved toward a point midway between the cat and his horse. He walked casually and made no sudden moves that might provoke the mountain lion into attacking. If he could he would avoid a fight.

The lion lowered itself even further and hissed.

"You don't know how lucky you are," Fargo said. "If I don't run you off, my pinto is liable to kick your fool head in." And he wasn't kidding. A grown stallion was more than a match for any mountain lion that ever lived. Once he'd even witnessed a battle between a wild stallion and a young grizzly that had ended in a tie but not before the grizzly had acquired more lumps on its thick skull than there were peaks in the Rockies.

"Mosey along, stupid," he goaded it and halted not twenty feet from the beast. He knew he could draw and put two or three slugs into the lion before it reached him, but he wished he held his Sharps. A Colt was a dandy man-stopper, and it could bring down most game at short distances, but for sheer power there was no beating the rifle. A single well-placed shot from a Sharps could drop a bull buffalo or a grizzly in its tracks.

Snarling viciously the mountain lion took a few creeping steps nearer. Its tail lashed angrily.

"Last warning," Skye said.

The lion inched forward once more.

As if the Colt was an extension of his arm, Fargo streaked the revolver out and banged off two shots, the slugs smacking into the ground in front of the cat's face and spewing dirt into its eyes.

Finally the mountain lion got the hint. Whirling faster than a striking snake, it bounded to the top of the gully and vanished over the rim.

Fargo walked to the Ovaro and rubbed its neck. "Some animals, it seems, don't have any more sense than some people I've met."

The Ovaro bobbed its head, as if agreeing, and vigilantly watched the top of the gully in case its nemesis should reappear.

"I doubt it will bother us again," Fargo commented. "By sunup it'll be feeding on a mule deer or maybe a young pronghorn." He returned to the fire and fed a handful of small branches into the flames, then tugged off his boots and eased onto his back. As a precaution he aligned the Sharps on one side of him and the Colt on the other and wearily closed his eyes. There was always a slim possibility the lion would come back, but he trusted the stallion to wake him up. The horse could hear and smell far better than any man, and on more occasions than he could count it had alerted him to danger in time to save both their hides.

In no time he was sound asleep.

Warm sunlight on his face awakened Fargo as the golden orb crested the eastern horizon and painted the sky in striking hues of pink and orange. He yawned, stretched, and sat up, feeling the morning chill and pining for a cup of hot coffee. Instead he made do with water and more jerky.

Soon he was saddled up and riding to the northwest. He noticed the huge tracks of the big cat leading westward. After that he saw no tracks of man or beast for almost an hour when he came on the spoor of a small herd of deer. There were fewer trees now and the land was much drier. Although the terrain was generally flat there were plenty of low hills and ridges plus enough gullies, washes, and ravines to make his ride interesting.

He constantly scoured the country for Indians. The Shoshones, who often hunted in this region, were basically friendly, but the Bannocks had been known to cause trouble now and then. And war parties of the fearsome Blackfeet sometimes ventured into the area. Should he encounter them he'd be hard pressed to stay alive.

Not a day's ride south of him lay the Oregon Trail, the rutted track followed by the countless wagon trains filled with hardy settlers bound for the fertile Willamette Valley. He could have made the journey easier on himself by following the Trail, but he never had been one to stick to established routes when there was so much country to explore, so many natural wonders he had never seen.

Then, too, he knew his search would begin in earnest at Fort Hall. From there he would ride the Oregon Trail, if need be, and hope he found some clue along the way.

By the landmarks he figured he was close to Fort Hall, and he began scouting for the bottoms where the fort was situated. Built by a fur trader named Nathaniel Wyeth back in the 1830s, it later passed into the hands of the Hudson's Bay Company who hung on tenaciously until just four years ago when the fur trade dwindled to practically nothing. He'd heard there were a few diehards still trapping in the area, old-timers who refused to admit their way of life had come to an end.

Before noon he came over a ridge and there was Fort Hall below. Never intended as a military fortification, it consisted of a crude wooden rectangular stockade that enclosed several buildings. Smoke rose from a squat chimney on top of the longest of the structures and there were a half-dozen horses tied to a hitching post in front of the door. The gate stood wide open.

Fargo shucked the Sharps as he descended the slope. After the incident at the river he was taking no chances. There might be more of the lawless element at the fort and he wanted to dissuade them from giving him a hard time.

No one appeared or hailed him as he rode through the gate and up to the hitching post. A building behind him, he saw, was a stable where three horses occupied stalls. The smallest building, over in the corner, appeared to be the living quarters for whomever currently occupied the fort. He swung down, tied the reins to the post, and sauntered into the long building.

A haze of tobacco smoke hung in the warm air. To the left ran a wide counter the length of the building, a counter where the trappers had once piled their pelts for the fur company representative to examine but was now being used as a bar. In the middle of the floor was a row of tables and chairs. To the right were two closed doors.

Fargo halted just inside the door, the Sharps in his left hand, his right dangling near the Colt. There was a portly man wearing a filthy apron behind the counter. In front of it were two men sipping drinks. At a table sat four men playing cards. And at another table were two women in tight dresses who wore more war paint than a Cheyenne brave on the war path. All eyes were on him, taking his measure, and he noticed the youngest of the women smile knowingly as he ambled over to the counter and set the Sharps down with a distinct thud.

The portly barkeep smiled and came down the bar. "Howdy, mister. The name is Burke. What will be your pleasure?"

"Whiskey," Skye said.

"Sure thing," Burke responded and hesitated, apparently expecting Fargo to introduce himself. When the big man simply stared he turned on his heels and went to fill the order.

Fargo leaned on an elbow and gazed at the cardplayers. One of the men was a grizzled mountain man who held his cards so close to his chest he had to tilt them back to study them. The other three were dressed much like those at the river. One of them wore a black, wide-brimmed hat and an ivory-handled pistol, butt forward for a cross draw, in a holster on his left hip.

"Mind if we join you, mister?"

Skye shifted. The two men at the bar were both young, both friendly, both wearing their hair long and clothing typical of cowhands from down Texas way. "Not at all," he replied, and straightened as they slid their glasses down the counter to join him, their spurs jingling in unison.

"I'm Harkey," the shortest of the pair said and offered his right hand. "This here is Lester. We're from San Antonio."

"Pleased to meet you," Fargo said, shaking.

"We're on our way up to Oregon," Harkey revealed. "Got plumb tired of watchin' the hind ends of cattle for a livin' and figured we'd see if everything we've heard about Oregon is true." He studied Fargo for a moment. "You look like the sort of hombre who knows his way around. Ever been there?"

"A few times," Skye admitted.

Harkey leaned forward. "Is it all they claim? Is it true the grass is green all year long and the soil is so rich you can grow any kind of crop? Is it true it never snows and hardly ever gets hot? Is it paradise, like the newspapers say?"

The man named Lester chuckled. "Don't pay him no mind, mister. He's been askin' every soul we meet the same questions. Shows you what happens when you take a newspaper story as gospel."

Fargo grinned. These two might be young, but it wouldn't do to underestimate them. He'd visited Texas before and knew the kind of grueling work cowhands were required to perform. They contended with cantankerous cattle that would as soon gore them as be herded, with Comanches and rustlers and rattlers and weather so hot a man could die of thirst in a day if left stranded on the staked plains. Young, yes, but they were as hard as nails and as fierce as bobcats when riled. "I'd say the newspapers have exaggerated," he said and saw Harkey's features droop. "But not by much, for once. The Willamette Valley has some of the best farmland I've ever laid eyes on, and the weather is mild all year round."

Harkey breathed in relief. "Well dog my cats!" He

glanced at Lester. "See? I told you this is the smartest move we've ever made."

Their conversation was interrupted by the bartender. He deposited a glass of whiskey in front of Skye and rested his hands on the edge of the bar. "They were asking me about Oregon too," he offered. "They figure to take up farming out there."

"Farmin' or whatever," Harkey amended. "Just so we can make a livin'." He took a swallow of his drink. "With the money we've saved, I reckon we can homestead and maybe find us some pretty wives from among all them settlers."

Fargo happened to be looking at Burke when the Texan mentioned the money, and he couldn't help but notice the bartender's eyes narrow slightly, then flick toward the table where the card game was being played. Almost immediately Burke caught himself and continued to listen to Harkey.

"Yes, sir. I'm lookin' forward to havin' a home of my own and a passel of younguns to drive me crazy. If I keep my nose clean and work hard I can be a big man in the territory before I'm through."

Lester laughed. "If talkin' counts, you might wind up president."

The barkeep coughed. "Are you boys planning to stay over tonight? There are a couple of spare bunks in the shack."

"No thanks," Lester said. "The sooner I get Harkey to Oregon, the sooner my ears get a rest."

Burke shrugged. "Suit yourselves. You'd likely have a better time at Killian's Trading Post anyhow."

The old man at the table, who had been intently watching the man with the black hat deal, glanced sharply at the counter and frowned.

"I didn't know there's a trading post hereabouts," Harkey mentioned.

"Me neither," Fargo said.

Burke fidgeted, then nodded. "Not many folks know about it yet because it just opened for business about three months ago. Takes time for word to spread along the Trail."

"What makes Killian's so special?" Lester asked.

"Better whiskey, for one thing. And five of the best-looking women you're likely to find this side of New Orleans," Burke said and lowered his voice. "Take my word for it. You'll have the time of your lives if you pay Killian's a visit."

"We'll give it some thought," Lester said.

Fargo raised his whiskey to his lips and gazed into the mirror behind the counter. Now why, he asked himself, would the proprietor of a rundown trading post send some of his few customers to his only competitor? Before he could give it much thought an angry shout drew his attention to the card game.

"I saw you that time!" the mountain man bellowed, jabbing a gnarled finger at the man in the black hat. "You dealt from the bottom of the deck, Curry."

Everyone had fallen silent. The two women rose and moved closer to the bar, out of harm's way should gunfire erupt.

"You're mistaken, Peterson," the tall man with the fancy pistol responded coldly, lowering his cards to the table to free his right hand for action.

"Like hell I am," Peterson snapped. "I've had my suspicions for some time and now I've caught you. I want all my money back and I want it now."

Curry was unruffled. He smiled and glanced at the other two players. "Some fools don't have the brains God gave a jackass." Slowly, almost nonchalantly, he eased his chair back and rested his right hand on his lap within easy reach of his revolver. "No one accuses me of being a cheat," he told the mountain man.

"I'm accusing you," Peterson snapped, refusing to be cowed. "You're a tinhorn, just like the rest of the wild bunch you ride with. And your boss is the worst of the lot."

"I'll make a point of telling him you said so," Curry responded.

"You do that," Peterson said, leaning nearer to the table, his left hand holding his cards, his right hand at the table's edge. "I'm not afeared of him or you or any of your crowd. You figured you could ride in here and take over the territory, but you're wrong. Folks won't stand for it."

"What folks?" Curry asked, smirking. "There are no settlements within hundreds of miles. Just this two-bit

23

fort and a few old bastards like you who don't know enough to curl up and die when their time comes." His smirk broadened. "And your time has come."

One of the other players, a rail of a man who had a Colt stuck under his belt to the right of the big silver buckle, cackled and slapped the table top. "All right! Let me do it, Curry. I've been itchin' to put this geezer in his place."

The third player grinned and nodded.

Peterson glanced contemptuously at each of them. "Three against one, huh? I should have known none of you polecats would fight fair."

"You want fair, I'll give you fair," the lean one said and stood, his right hand held an inch from his gun, his cruel features glowing with wicked expectation. "If you have a gun, go for it."

"I ain't no damned gunman, Shanks, and you know it," Peterson replied.

"That's your tough luck," Shanks said, taking a step to one side. He laughed lightly, then stabbed his hand for his gun, a gleam of triumph in his eyes as his fingers closed on the six-shooter and he started to draw, a gleam that changed to full unconsciousness an instant later when a tremendous blow struck him on the back of the head. Wordlessly he fell, sprawling beside the table.

No one else moved. No one uttered a sound. They all stared at the big man in buckskins who held the Sharps he had just used so effectively in both hands with the barrel pointing squarely at Curry's chest, and they all heard the click of the hammer being cocked. The third man at the table began to rise, as if intending to draw, but something about the big man's expression froze him where he sat.

"Peterson wants his money back. Give it to him," Fargo directed.

"Like hell we will!" the third man barked. "Who do you think you are meddling in our affair like this? You might have busted Shank's skull hitting him with that stock like you did."

"I doubt he'd notice the difference," Fargo said, keeping the Sharps trained on Curry.

The third man tensed.

Curry twisted ever so slightly. "Don't do anything

dumb, Carl, or you'll answer to me. This hombre means business." Carl relaxed, his anger obvious. "Never figured I'd see the day when you'd back down from any man," he muttered.

"A good poker player always knows when to fold," Curry said and faced Fargo. "He knows there will always be other times when he'll hold the winning hand." He paused. "Something to keep in mind, mister."

"The money," Fargo reminded him.

Curry began separating his winnings into two piles. The clink of coins was the only sound in the whole building until Shanks groaned. "Here you go, Peterson," Curry said and shoved a pile at the mountain man. "Nine dollars should about do it."

"Much obliged, you son of a bitch."

Again Curry looked at Fargo. And while his face was composed, a fiery rage blazed deep within his eyes. "We'll meet again, mister. I promise you."

"Looking forward to it," Fargo said.

Curry rose slowly, his arms out from his sides, and turned toward the door. For a heartbeat his gaze lingered on Burke, and then he was walking away. "Carl, bring Shanks," he ordered over his shoulder.

"Why me?" Carl responded.

"Because if you don't I'll kill you."

Carl came out of his chair as if jabbed by a scorpion and stepped around the table. Squatting, he grunted as he hoisted Shanks over a shoulder and hurried out after Curry.

Fargo waited until he heard the drumming of hoofs before he let the hammer down on the Sharps and walked back to the bar to take a swallow of whiskey. The liquid burned all the way down his throat and warmed his insides, easing his tight stomach muscles. For a second there he had anticipated gunplay. Carl and Shanks hadn't worried him in the least, but Curry had been another story. The man reminded him of that mountain lion—all muscle and meanness and as shrewd as they came. And probably as fast as chained lightning.

"Whooee!" Harkey declared, giving Skye a friendly clap on the shoulder. "You like to dabble in gore, don't you, pardner? I'm not much for shootin' scrapes, myself, but I was fixin' to back your play just for the hell of it."

"I appreciate it," Fargo said.

Lester poked a finger into Harkey's arm. "Give a man some warning, why don't you?"

"What's stuck in your craw?" Harkey asked in surprise.

"I'm your pard, ain't I? If you threw in with this he-bear I'd have to throw in with you, but I'd be the last to clear leather because you didn't let me know. Next time use your head."

Fargo looked at the bartender, who was staring at him intently. "Something on your mind, Burke?"

"Just that I wouldn't want to be in your boots. Curry isn't the type to forgive and forget."

"He's not the only one," Fargo said and felt his stomach rumble. "Any chance of getting a hot meal?"

Burke nodded. "Peterson brought in a buck fresh this morning. Traded it for some whiskey." He wiped his hands on his apron. "I can rustle up a thick steak, some potatoes and greens, and a couple of slices of bread. Will that do?"

"Just fine," Fargo said, his mouth watering at the prospect of eating a full meal again. "How much?"

"The eats are on me, mister," Peterson interjected from the card table. "The least I can do after what you done."

Fargo turned. "Thanks. Mind if I join you."

"Not at all," the mountain man said, indicating the chair Carl had occupied.

Taking his drink and the Sharps, and with a nod to the Texans, Fargo strolled over and sat down. He was now facing the bar and could see the open front door. Should Curry or the others come back they wouldn't take him by surprise. "You took a chance bracing those three like that."

"A man ain't much of a man if he don't stick up for himself," Peterson replied. "Besides, I would have taken at least one of them buzzards with me when I cashed in." He snickered and pointed at his lap.

Bending forward, Fargo saw a gleaming bowie knife and grinned. Many of the old-timers were hellions with blades, and he didn't doubt for a minute that Peterson would have put up a terrific fight. "Have you been in these parts long?"

"Came out here after beaver back in '38 and stayed ever since. Never planned to, but the first time I laid eyes on the Salmon River Mountains north of here I knew I'd found the place where they'd plant me one day. Hard to say why. Just a feeling, was all."

"You come down here often?"

"Now and then. Used to be a lot of trappers here before the Hudson's Bay Company pulled freight. Some of them were my friends. We'd play cards and drink until we couldn't see straight and frolic with the ladies for a day or two at a stretch," Peterson said wistfully and sighed. "Those were the days."

Fargo let his voice drop so no one else could overhear. "You wouldn't happen to have been here when the Moreland party came through on their way to Oregon?"

"With a wagon train, were they?"

"Only four wagons, all told. Moreland was the leader. He's a farmer from Ohio. Had his wife along, a small brunette partial to wearing red bonnets, and two kids, both boys."

"Doesn't sound like anyone I saw," Peterson said. "But then I'm not here all the time. Wagon trains stop by pretty regular, but not all of them do. Some go on by. Could have been that the Moreland bunch was one of them."

"I know they stopped here," said Fargo.

"Oh?" Peterson scratched his bushy beard. "How long ago was this?"

"Not quite two months ago."

"Hmmmm. Let me think on it a spell. I came down from the mountains about that time and there were some pilgrims here, but I didn't pay much attention to them. The settlers tend to keep to themselves." He snickered. "Most of 'em think us mountain men are downright crazy."

Disappointed, Fargo sat back and glanced at the door. His food would arrive soon, and he should take care of the Ovaro before he ate. "Who runs the stable?"

"Who else? Burke. He charges too much but he does have good feed on hand."

"Tell him I'll be right back if he shows with my grub,"

Fargo said and rose. The women were watching him and whispering as he went to the door. After the dim interior he had to squint in the bright sunlight, and he paused to let his eyes adjust. It was then, as he reached up to pull the brim of his hat lower, that he spotted a sparkle of light near the fort gate.

A second later a rifle boomed.

3

In the fleeting interval between spotting the light and the blast of the gun Fargo launched himself into a dive. He hit the ground hard on his elbows as a slug smacked into the doorjamb, then rolled to the right, away from the horses, and swept to his knees with the Sharps tucked against his right shoulder. He saw a figure in the shadows beside the gate and hastily fired. Wood chips flew from the gate and the figure bolted.

Skye stood and sprinted forward, drawing the Colt as he rose. He thumbed back the hammer, eager for another shot at the bushwhacker, and reached the corner of the gate safely. From beyond the stockade came the noise of a horse galloping off. "Damn!" he fumed and ran out.

Thirty yards off was a familiar form on a dun. The man whipped his horse frantically, trying to put more distance behind him.

"Not this time," Fargo said softly, holstering the .44. He took a cartridge from his pocket and worked the trigger guard like a lever, then fed the cartridge into the Sharps.

The bushwhacker was fifty yards off now.

Skye returned the breechblock to the closed position and slowly lifted the rifle to his shoulder. He let the fleeing figure keep going as if he was letting out the line on a hooked fish. Seventy-five yards separated them. Then one hundred. At one hundred and fifty yards the rider reached the base of a hill and looked back, grinning.

There was no need to adjust the sights. The slug would drop very little at such a range. Skye took careful aim on the very center of the bushwhacker's face, elevated the rifle a fraction to compensate, held his breath to steady the barrel, and fired.

Propelled by ninety grains of powder, the slug ripped into Carl between the eyes and blew out the back of his head in a spray of hair and blood. He died still grinning and toppled with his arms out-flung. The horse never slowed down and was soon out of sight over the hill.

Footsteps pounded as Skye lowered the Sharps and replaced the spent cartridge. When he turned they were all there, even Burke and the women, staring at the distant prone body in amazement.

"What the hell happened, mister?" Harkey asked.

"Carl didn't know to leave well enough alone," Fargo replied, heading back into the fort.

Peterson chuckled heartily. "I wish I'd of seen it. That bastard had it coming."

"Aren't you going to bury him?" Burke inquired.

"Buzzards have to eat too, don't they?" Fargo rejoined. He walked to the Ovaro and led the stallion to the stable, heedless of the stares of the others. After stripping everything off and draping his saddle over a rail, he put the Ovaro in a stall, found a feed bag, and gave the pinto plenty of oats, a rarity so far from civilization. He left his bedroll by the stall but took his saddlebags with him when he returned to the trading post. A plate heaped with food awaited him as did a steaming pot of coffee.

Peterson was playing a game of solitaire. He glanced up and nodded at a cup in front of him. "Hope you don't mind, but I helped myself."

"Drink all you want," Fargo said, taking his seat. He leaned the Sharps against the table and put the saddlebags on the floor at his feet.

"You must live a charmed life. Some folks considered Carl to be a good shot."

"Not good enough," Skye said, picking up his fork and knife. He cut into the steak and forked a juicy piece into his mouth, then methodically chewed, savoring the taste.

"You look like a man starved for a decent meal," Peterson commented.

Skye gazed at the two women standing near the counter. "That's not all I'm starved for."

The mountain man snorted. "If you want my advice,

the young one, Rosie, is the best. She likes her work and doesn't put on airs."

"Why do they stick around here when they'd make more money in Oregon or back in Denver?"

"I don't rightly know. They were at Killian's for a while, then about a week ago they showed up here and asked Burke if they could work for him until they saved enough money to get them back to Denver. Seems they didn't like the way Killian treated them."

"What do you know about this Killian?"

The mountain man glanced at the bar, where Burke was talking to the Texans, then leaned over the table and spoke almost in a whisper. "If you run into him, you watch yourself. He's as contrary as a rattler and more vicious than a rabid wolf. They say he's killed upwards of twenty men and I believe it. All you have to do is look into his eyes to know he'd kill his own mother if she crossed him."

"Have you been to his trading post?"

Peterson scowled. "Once, and that was enough. His whiskey and women were so overpriced it was ridiculous. And I suspect the card games are rigged though I couldn't figure out how."

Fargo chewed while digesting the information. He'd run across men like Killian before, greedy, unscrupulous types who would do anything to make a dollar. "Does he get much business?"

"More than you'd expect. He has a sign posted near the Oregon Trail, and it draws in the pilgrims like rotten apples draw flies. Every so often one of 'em winds up being gunned down or knifed but it doesn't stop the next wagon train from stopping over for a spell."

"I think I'll pay Killian a visit soon."

"You just remember my warning. And don't let any of his men stand behind you, if you get my meaning."

"Curry works for him?"

Peterson nodded. "He's Killian's right-hand man. Best with a gun I ever did see. And Killian has a small army of owl-hoots with him. Twelve or fifteen, I reckon."

"Why does the operator of a trading post need so many gunmen?" Skye mused aloud.

"My thinking exactly," Peterson said, looking at him. "Which is another reason I ain't never been back there."

31

Fargo ate the rest of his meal in silence, thinking about the job he had been hired to do. It might turn out to be a lot more complicated than he had imagined. The next step would be to go to Killian's Trading Post and see what he could uncover, and since Killian and company weren't likely to be very open to strangers, he would have to keep his eyes and ears open at all times and never let down his guard for an instant. It was possible that Moreland had gone on to Killian's from Burke's, and if so there might be a clue there.

As he was finishing the last of the delicious steak he saw the young woman sashay toward him, her black hair swaying with each stride, her green eyes sparkling.

"Howdy, mister. The name is Rosie. Mind if I join you?"

Skye motioned at the empty chair across from him. "Be my guest."

Rosie pulled out the chair and sat down. She glanced at the empty plate, and the tip of her tongue touched her lower lip. "Anyone ever tell you that you pack away food like a bear about to go into hibernation?"

"Are you hungry?" Fargo asked.

"I could use a bite to eat," Rosie answered, leaning back and squaring her slender shoulders and in the process revealing more of her ample bosom.

"Burke!" Fargo called out. "Another meal for the lady here, on me."

"Give me five minutes."

Peterson suddenly stood. "Well, if you folks will excuse me I have to go tend to my mule." He looked at Fargo. "Again, thanks for the help. I'll pay for your meal on the way out." He smiled at Rosie and walked off.

"Mind telling me your name, mister?" Rosie asked. "It isn't often I get to meet a real gentleman and I'd like to know who I'm dealing with."

"Fargo."

"That's it? Just Fargo?"

Skye nodded. There was no sense in revealing his full name just yet. "You ever hear about what curiosity did to the cat?"

"I can take a hint," Rosie said, grinning. "And I know how it is west of the Mississippi. A lot of men are on the dodge for one reason or another and go by a nickname or a phony name." She cocked her head. "Are you on the dodge?"

"I thought you could take a hint?" Fargo said.

"The Copen clan are famous for their hard heads," Rosie said and laughed. "That's how I wound up here in this godforsaken fort in the middle of the wilderness."

"Copen is your last name?"

"Yep. Born and raised in Philadelphia, and then one day about four years ago I decided I knew more than my parents and went off to see the world on my own," Rosie related. "They always told me the West is no place for a woman to try and make it by herself, but I wouldn't listen. So now . . . ," she said and left the sentence unfinished, sadness sagging her features.

"You could always go back to Philadelphia."

"And give my mother the satisfaction of crowing about how she was right all the time? No, sir. I'd rather go hungry than eat crow."

Fargo admired her spunk but felt sorry for her nonetheless. Countless girls just like her had left their homes seeking a better life or gone off for the thrill of it and found themselves living on the wrong side of the tracks, forced to make money the only way they could. He guessed her age to be twenty-one or twenty-two, certainly not much older. "Maybe one day the right man will come along," he said.

"I hope so. When he does, I'll do him proud," Rosie said, then averted her gaze and coughed to clear her throat. "Hell, what are we talking like this for? I want to have some fun, eat my full, drink a little, and show you a good time. Any objections?"

He stared at her breasts thrusting against the fabric of her dress, and at her full red lips, and shook his head. "A man would have to be crazy to say yes."

For the next hour they made small talk. Fargo ordered drinks for both of them and sipped his while Rosie ate and gabbed on about her childhood and her travels since leaving Philadelphia. He became attentive when she mentioned running into Ben Killian back in Denver and listened closely as she told how Killian had approached her and several other doves about working for him at a trading post he was going to establish.

"Little did I know," Rosie said. "He never said nothing about it being in the Snake River area. If he had I wouldn't have come. This has got to be the most desolate region there is."

"I've seen worse."

"Really? Hardly matters, I guess, since he cheated Flo and me. When I objected he beat me within an inch of my life. So we came here."

"Doesn't take much of a man to hit a woman," Fargo said, irritation flaring. He never had liked men who used their fists to cow their wives or sweethearts into doing whatever they wanted. It gave him yet another reason to dislike Ben Killian, and he hadn't even met the man.

"Killian likes beating people up. Men, women, makes no nevermind to him. Once I saw him tangle with three men from a wagon train and knock out all three. He's broken more bones than most ten men. If he ever challenges you to a fight you'd be smart to turn him down."

"I'll remember that," Fargo promised. He ordered another drink for each of them and sipped at his while she wrapped up her meal. The other, older woman was leaning on the counter, in conversation with Lester. Harkey still talked to Burke. "How would I get to Killian's from here?"

"Easy. Ride southwest until you hit the Trail, then go west a couple of miles. There's a big sign nailed to a tree. You can't miss it."

"How far from the Trail to Killian's?"

"Oh, not more than a mile or so. He built it at the mouth of a gorge. Posts lookouts up on top to let him know when wagons are coming."

Interesting, Fargo thought. The lookouts could also let Killian know when unwanted company was riding in. The man seemed to be a thorough planner and wasn't to be taken lightly.

"Thanks for the eats," Rosie said, giving her trim tummy a little pat. "I'm afraid I made a pig of myself. Does it show?"

"Just in the right places."

She grinned devilishly and sighed, expanding her dress until it threatened to burst. "Flo and I happen to have part of the shack out back all to ourselves. Would you care to walk me over there and I'll show you?"

"My pleasure, ma'am," Skye said with exaggerated civility and rose. He pulled out her chair for her, then went over to the bar to pay Burke for her meal. Farther down the counter Flo and the Texans were talking in low voices.

The bartender took the money and winked. "Enjoy yourself, mister. I hear she's a firebrand in the sack, but she never will put out for me. Can't understand why."

"There's no accounting for taste," Fargo said dryly, and with Rosie at his side he walked to the front door. "Hold it," he cautioned and peered out to see if the coast was clear. The compound was deserted except for the horses at the hitching post. He didn't think Killian's men would try to bushwhack him again so soon, but he'd learned a long time ago never to take an enemy for granted.

"Is it all right?" Rosie asked.

"Appears so. Let's go," Skye said, taking her elbow. The Sharps was in his left hand, his saddlebags over his left shoulder.

"I want to tell you it did my heart good to see Carl get his due," Rosie commented as they strolled across the open ground toward the shack.

"You didn't like him?"

"Hell, no. Not him or any of the bunch that ride for Killian. They're all animals," she responded. "All but Curry. Believe it or not, he was the only one who treated us girls right. Never pawed us or tried to slip a hand between our legs without an invitation."

"And Killian?"

"All he's interested in is money. Becoming rich is an obsession with him. Shanks once confided in me that Killian keeps a safe in his office at the back of the trading post. If anyone so much as touches it, Killian shoots them dead."

"Does that include Curry?" Fargo probed, glad for the opportunity to uncover critical information. The more he could learn now would be to his advantage when he paid Killian's a visit. If there were any more surprises like the lookouts, he wanted to learn beforehand rather than the hard way.

"Oh, no," Rosie answered. "I think Curry is the only man alive Killian is a bit afraid of. Killian bosses the others around like they're trash, which they are, but he never raises his voice to Curry. He knows better."

As they approached the shack, Fargo saw there were two doors, one on the right and another around the corner on the left. Rosie angled toward the left-hand door.

"This is our side. Burke has the other," she said and giggled. "Sometimes I think he listens at the wall when we're with customers."

"If he tries it with me he'll lose an ear."

"Don't worry. After the way you made Curry back down, Burke isn't about to cross you."

The interior of the shack was about what Fargo expected—cramped, grimy, and drafty. There was no window to let in light so Rosie lit a lantern on a small table in a corner. The two beds were positioned on opposite sides. One had been neatly made, the other was disheveled, and it was on the neat one that Rosie took a seat. "Make yourself comfortable, big man."

Fargo first threw the bolt to lock the door, then stepped to the bed and sat down next to her. The springs creaked loudly and the mattress was no thicker than paper.

"Burke got these beds from Killian. I'm afraid they're not much."

"How soon before you can leave here?" Skye inquired, bracing his rifle against the wall and putting the saddlebags on the floor.

"If we had twenty dollars we could pay for passage to Fort Laramie and from there to Denver."

Skye stood, reached into a pocket, and pulled out the advance he had been paid. He peeled off twenty dollars and handed it over to the astonished Rosie. "I expect you to be gone within the week."

A squeal of delight burst from Rosie, and she leaped erect, clutching the money so tightly it crumpled. She touched the bills to her lips, then stared inquisitively at him. "I don't understand, Fargo. Why are you doing this for us? We don't know you."

"Haven't you heard? Never look a gift horse in the mouth."

Rosie impulsively threw her slim arms around his neck and pecked him on the cheek. "I can never thank you enough." She drew back, crossed to a shabby dresser, and deposited the money in a small jewelry box inside.

Her back was to him, and Skye saw her hands rise to her neck and slowly lower. When she pivoted a minute later he was pleasantly surprised to see she had exposed both breasts. A seductive smile curled her lips as she glided toward him like a cat in heat, a hungry gleam in her eyes, her twin mounds jiggling temptingly.

"I aim to make sure you never forget this," Rosie said huskily.

Skye was about to reply when he heard a faint scratching noise outside the door. She heard it too and whirled, her arms covering her breasts. Darting to the door, he drew the Colt and thumbed back the hammer as he threw the bolt. With a quick jerk he yanked the door wide open and rushed out, swiveling right and left, ready to fire.

The compound was empty.

Puzzled, he walked to the end of the shack nearest the stockade but saw no one in the narrow space. He carefully let down the hammer and twirled the .44 into its holster, then went back inside and closed the door behind him.

"Anything?" Rosie asked.

"All clear," Fargo said, shoving the bolt home again.

"Maybe it was a chipmunk or a squirrel. They're always scampering around the fort. The squirrels even climb the walls sometimes."

"Maybe."

Rosie grinned, dropped her hands, and walked right up to him, pressing her ripe body against his. "Now where were we?"

4

Fargo rested his hands on her firm buttocks and kissed her. She opened her mouth to admit his tongue, then entwined her own with his in slick, silken circles. Her warm breath, exhaled through her nostrils in a sort of fluttering sigh, tingled his cheek. He squeezed her bottom gently for a while before grinding her nether mound into his groin.

Rosie moaned and squirmed deliciously, her fingers roving over his ears and hair. She removed his hat and without opening her eyes tossed it to one side.

Fargo's sexual hunger was fully aroused. After being forced to abstain during the long ride from Denver, he desired her with the same intensity as a starving man desires morsels of food. His hands traced a path from her buttocks to the middle of her back, then slid around in front, and he cupped both of her breasts. They swelled under his expert massaging, the twin nipples becoming hard points as he slowly fueled her lust.

On her part, Rosie broke their kiss to nibble and lick his throat and ears. She had to stand on her toes to reach his earlobes, her hips grinding into him the whole time.

He suddenly stooped and scooped her into his brawny arms. She grinned as he carried her to the bed and placed her on her back. Her hand reached out to press on the prominent bulge in his pants, and her grin broadened into a pleased smile.

"My, you're a big one."

Fargo smiled. "Think you can handle it?"

For an answer Rosie looped her arms around his neck and pulled him down to bestow a passionate kiss. Her right hand languidly stroked his erect manhood.

Fargo leaned on his left elbow so he could strip off his

gunbelt and loosen his pants. He began removing her dress, dallying at each button, heightening the suspense. When he slipped a hand under the dress and ran his palm over her stomach, Rosie quivered and arched her back.

Soon the dress was off, and Fargo could admire Rosie in all her naked glory. She possessed a marvelous body, with huge breasts, a narrow waist, and shapely thighs. Her skin, pale from infrequent exposure to the sun, was as smooth as the finest silk money could buy. And she gave off a tantalizing scent that he found tremendously stimulating.

He cast off his shirt, boots, and pants, and lay flush with her. Her nipples dug into his chest, her pubic hair brushed his loins. He locked his lips on hers while his hands savored her delights.

"Mmmmmm," Rosie groaned, her nails digging lightly into his upper arms.

For the longest time Fargo contented himself with rubbing her inner thighs and occasionally rubbing her slit. She was soaking wet and as hot as a furnace, eager for his organ. He slowly lowered himself down her body, his mouth busy at her throat, her breasts, and her stomach in succession. At length he came to the junction of her thighs and licked each one.

Rosie gasped and bent her legs at the knees, then clamped her thighs to his ears as she braced both hands on the top of his head and pushed his mouth into her moist womanhood. He knew what she wanted and accommodated her, his tongue darting into her innermost recesses and flicking out again over the throbbing knob at the top of her slit. She trembled and cooed and pulled on his hair as if about to tear it loose by the roots.

"That's nice, big man! Keep it up! You make me feel sooooooo good!"

Fargo licked until his mouth and chin were dripping wet from her love juices, and his tongue began to ache. Reluctantly he pried her thighs from his head and rose on his knees so he could touch the tip of his shaft to her fiery hole.

"Yes!" Rosie prompted. "Give it to me!"

He slipped into her as easily as a knife into its sheath, taking it slow for the first several inches and then ramming his manhood to the hilt. She squealed and flung her arms out, her mouth parted seductively.

"Aaaaaaah yes! Oh! Oh!"

His mouth swooped to her lovely nipples, and he tongued them and their light pink areolas. She grasped his behind and helped him pump back and forth, his pole plunging repeatedly into the core of her womanhood. The friction generated increasing heat, and he felt beads of sweat form.

"Oooohhhhh!" Rosie cried. "Do you feel it? Do you feel it?"

Fargo was too busy tonguing her breasts to respond. He squeezed them, then put his hands on her hips and straightened. Her dripping portal clung to his organ as he started to stroke in earnest. His blood raced, his temples pounded, and he drank in the sight of her wriggling form, her full mounds bobbing as her bottom rocked up and down.

When the explosion came he wasn't expecting it. He'd intended to pace himself, to prolong their delight, but her reaction aroused him beyond human endurance. She abruptly began bucking like a wild mare, and her eyes snapped wide in amazement. Her flat stomach slapped into his as she elevated her bottom to meet each thrust.

"Pound me, honey! Oh, pound me to pieces!"

He held off for all of ten seconds. Then he experienced a familiar constriction in his throat and face, and a moment later his manhood was on the brink of spending. Not yet! his mind cried, and he gritted his teeth and rammed into her like a bull into a willing heifer.

"That's it!" Rosie wailed, beside herself, her head tossing back and forth, her arms waving wildly.

Fargo dimly heard the bed creaking. He thought he heard a faint sound like the closing of a door but paid no attention, swept up as he was in the ecstasy of the instant.

"Now!" Rosie screeched. "Oh, Lord! Now, big man!"

Fargo couldn't have held back any longer if he wanted to. He let go, his pole spurting mightily, feeling the exquisite spasms inside of her as she reciprocated and attained her own peak. They coupled almost savagely for minutes on end. Eventually they slowed, both of them breathing heavily, both of them slick with sweat. He slumped down on top of her, using her breasts for a pillow, then rolled onto his left side and embraced her.

"Wonderful," Rosie breathed. "Just wonderful."

He pecked her on the tip of her nose and closed his eyes, thinking he would rest a short while. But the long, arduous trip had taken more out of him than he figured, and the next thing he knew he was opening his eyes again, and he instinctively knew he had slept for hours. His skin was cool, covered with goose bumps. Rosie snored softly.

Skye sat up, taking care not to disturb her. He swiftly dressed and strapped on the Colt, glancing at the bottom of the door as he notched the belt buckle. Where earlier there had been a line of light there was now dark shadow. And sure enough, after he grabbed his rifle and saddlebags and quietly eased the door open, he discovered twilight had descended and night wasn't far off.

He left Rosie to her sleep and softly closed the door. The rest had refreshed him immensely, and he felt invigorated as he strolled toward the trading post. He paused at the hitching rail when he realized two of the horses that had been there when he arrived were gone.

Inside all was still. Flo sat glumly at a table idly playing with the cards. Burke was behind the bar at the near end, reading an old magazine. There was no sign of the two Texans.

Fargo walked over to the table where Flo sat and put down the Sharps and his saddlebags. She glanced up and gave him a kindly smile.

"I was beginning to think you'd stay in there all night."

"There's something I need to know," Fargo said so low that the proprietor couldn't possibly hear him. "Did Burke leave at any time while we were gone?"

Flo stiffened, nervously looked at Burke, then nodded once. "He left right after those fellows from Texas rode out. Said he'd be back in a bit, but he was gone for about ten minutes. Came back in grinning like the cat that just ate a mouse."

"Do you happen to know where the Texans went?"

"Yep. Burke talked them into visiting Killian's Trading Post. I don't think Lester was too keen on going, but Harkey had his mind set, and those boys always do everything together."

"Thanks," Fargo said. "You might want to leave now."

Flo scrutinized his face. "No thanks. I want to stay and see it."

"Duck down if he pulls a gun," Skye advised. Pivoting, he stepped to the bar. Burke made a great show of being intently interested in his beat-up copy of *Police News*, a publication out of New York City that stressed sensational, gory crimes. "Anything interesting?" he asked, putting both hands on top of the counter.

Burke finally glanced at him and grinned. "It says here they found a woman who had her face beaten to a pulp with a hammer. Imagine that. Care to read the story?"

"No thanks. I'd rather do the same to you," Skye said, and before Burke could guess what he was about he reached over, gripped him by the front of the shirt, and pulled, every muscle straining as he hauled the startled man around the end of the bar.

"What the hell!" Burke blurted.

With a swipe of his left hand Fargo knocked the magazine to the floor, then he delivered a punch to the gut that doubled Burke at the waist. It was like punching a pillow there was so much fat around the man's middle.

"Why?" Burke blubbered, staggering.

"You know why," Fargo said, and kicked Burke's legs out from under him.

Yelping, Burke crashed onto his back and made no move to get up. He clasped his enormous stomach, glaring wickedly. "What the hell are you doing? You have no right to treat me like this."

Fargo leaned over to grip Burke's shirt again. "I don't like being spied on," he said harshly and lifted Burke off the floor.

"I don't know what you're talking about!"

"Like hell you don't," Fargo said and hit him full on the mouth. Burke tottered rearward and collided with a table. He tried to catch himself but went down, taking the table with him. Fargo stalked forward.

"Now you hold on, mister!" Burke screamed, extending his right arm, palm out. "You don't have any proof that I spied on you."

"I don't need proof."

Burke scrambled to his feet, blood trickling from a

corner of his mouth. "This ain't right, damn you. I won't take being beaten like this."

"Then defend yourself," Fargo suggested grimly. "Please." To his surprise, the man did just that, springing at him while raining a barrage of blows with his fleshy fists. Fargo raised his arms in time to deflect several of the punches, then jabbed a left to the jaw that caused Burke to rock on his heels.

"Damn you all to hell!"

Fargo adopted a boxing stance and waded into the Peeping Tom, flicking a right that clipped Burke on the jaw and a left that bruised Burke's cheek. But the man wasn't a coward. Burke lashed out clumsily, his heavy bulk adding power to his swings, some of which landed. Fargo took a punch to the chin that rattled his teeth and another in the ribs that lanced his chest with pain. But Burke wasn't a skilled fighter and didn't know when to press an advantage. By backing off a pace Skye recovered sufficiently from each blow to wade in again.

Flo had risen and was standing near the bar, aglow with excitement.

A punch narrowly missed Fargo's eye, and he countered with a right and left combination square on the jaw that sent Burke toppling onto a chair. The chair shattered and Burke sprawled among the broken pieces, too dazed to stand. "Now then," Fargo growled, straddling him and shoving his fist into the man's face. "How long were you spying on us?"

"I wasn't—" Burke began and received knuckles in the midsection for his lie.

"How long?" Fargo demanded. He started shaking the man as a wolf might shake its helpless prey.

"Stop!" Burke wailed. "Stop and I'll tell you!"

Releasing the shirt, Fargo straightened and moved to one side. "I'm listening."

"That's all I did, was listen," Burke said. "Honest to God. I didn't watch you or nothing." He gingerly touched his battered lips. "I do it now and then for entertainment. What harm is there in a little innocent fun?"

Fargo kicked him. He drew back his right boot and slammed it into Burke's groin, then stood back while Burke clutched himself and rolled from side to side, shaking in acute torment. "I should shoot you," he said.

43

"No!" Burke managed to scream. "Please, no! I'll never do it again! Please!"

"You'd better not. Rosie and Flo will be leaving soon, and if I hear of you bothering them again before they leave, I'll finish the job," Fargo warned and went to the table.

Burke curled into a ball, closed his eyes, and groaned, spittle flecking his thick lips.

"What was that about leaving?" Flo inquired, coming over.

"Go ask Rosie. She'll explain," Fargo answered. He retrieved the Sharps and his saddlebags and turned as she dashed out. Although strongly inclined to kick the bastard again, he reined in his temper and walked outside. Night blanketed the Snake River region and stars sparkled high in the sky.

He made for the stable. Originally he figured to ride to Killian's in the morning, but now he wanted to overtake the Texans if possible and either persuade them to change their minds or tag along with them. He had liked those two, and he didn't want to see them come to any harm. If Killian's was as rough as everyone claimed, they might run into trouble.

The Ovaro had eaten its fill and seemed disposed to stay in the stall where it was nice and warm. He got the stallion saddled, slid the Sharps into the scabbard, and led the pinto out into the cool night air. The door to the room the women shared was open a crack, and gay laughter wafted on the breeze.

He swung onto the stallion and departed the fort. Recalling Rosie's directions, he rode southwest, which took him to the same hill Carl had been about to climb when his shot brought the bushwhacker down. He found the area where the body should be, but it was gone. Halting, he scoured the ground. Either Burke had brought it back to the fort while he was with Rosie, or someone else had come along. He wondered if Peterson or the Texans had taken it yet could see no reason that they would.

Shrugging, he rode on, knowing sooner or later he would strike the Snake River. He was on the lookout for campfires since there was always the chance a passing wagon train had camped on the Oregon Trail. All he saw was a sea of darkness. He had to travel slowly in order to reduce the risk of the pinto stepping into a hole or rut and going down. Every seasoned frontiersman knew that any man foolish enough to ride at a full gallop on a moonless night had better have a damn good reason and have made his peace with his Maker. All it would take would be for one of the horse's hoofs to step into a prairie dog burrow or some other hole or rut and the rider could well end up with a broken neck.

He enjoyed the ride. But then he had always felt at home in the wild places, had always preferred the mountains and the plains of the West to all other areas. They drew him to them like a magnet drew iron. He couldn't wait to see what might lie over the next peak or beyond the far horizon. It accounted for his restless wanderlust, for why he could never hang his hat in one spot for more than a few days at a time without feeling an urge to saddle up and ride out.

Not that he would ever complain. He'd seen more sights than most ten men. Hell, more than most other scouts and explorers combined. Which explained how he knew the land between the Mississippi and the Pacific better than almost any man alive and why folks had taken to calling him the Trailsman.

A wolf howled to the northwest, interrupting his train of thought. He listened to the wavering call, stirred by its plaintive tone. Next to the throaty screech of a mountain lion and the yip of a coyote, few sounds so perfectly fit the wild country.

Over an hour later he spotted an oasis of light in the sea of darkness. As he drew nearer, the light separated into the distinct glows from a number of campfires. Even closer and he distinguished the unmistakable silhouettes of Conestogas and saw people moving about within the circle of wagons.

It was a wagon train camped near the Oregon Trail. They were bound to have posted sentries, pilgrims who might be a bit trigger-happy, so he prudently reined up a couple of dozen yards out and cupped his hands to his mouth. "Hello! Mind if I pay you a visit?"

A few men congregated between two wagons directly ahead and one of them replied.

"Come on in, stranger! And welcome!"

Fargo rode up to them and touched the brim of his hat

45

in greeting. There were four men waiting, three wearing homespun clothes so typical of farmers while the fourth was wearing jeans, a buckskin shirt, and a brown hat.

"Howdy," the man in the hat said. "I'm Varner, the wagon-boss." He motioned at the others. "These men are from Missouri. They're bound for Oregon."

"If you're hungry I'll have the wife rustle you up some grub," offered one of the farmers.

"Thanks, but I'm not staying," Fargo told him. "Have you had any Indian trouble on your way out?"

"Not a lick," Varner responded. "We ran into a band of Shoshones but they let us pass without causing a fuss after we gave them two head of cattle."

A farmer laughed. "And here we were so worried we'd be scalped alive before we reached Oregon! The most excitement we've had was when we tried to cross a flooded river and lost a wagon."

"Haven't run into too many people, white or red," chimed in a second Missourian. "Then we stopped here and since dark we've had more visitors than in a month of Sundays."

"Visitors?"

"Yep. There were two Texans who paid their respects a while ago, and before them there was a man from Killian's Trading Post who invited us to stop by."

"Any of your people go to the post?" Fargo inquired.

"Eight of our men did," Varner said. "They went to buy some supplies. We expect them back before too long."

"I'm headed there myself. If I see them I'll pass the word you're looking for them," Fargo said, turning the pinto to the west. "Have a safe trip," he added and hurried in search of Killian's. He didn't have far to look. A mile farther he spotted more lights, only these were on a hill to the north of the Trail.

A belt of thin forest bordered Killian's to the south. On one of those trees must be the sign Rosie had mentioned, but he didn't see it in the dark. He slanted through the forest until he spied a rise. Looking up he could make out five buildings in an oval basin and above the basin the inky outline of the gorge. Any lookouts posted on top were invisible.

He heard gruff laughter, the tinkle of glasses, and

someone playing the guitar. For a small trading post off the beaten track it was doing brisk business. The layout had been arranged with the long, low trading post structure itself partially blocking the mouth of the gorge. To the right of it were two cabins. To the left was another cabin and a building half the size of the post proper. Every one was brilliantly lit by lanterns within.

Fargo loosened the Colt in its holster and rode along the wide dirt track leading to the front door of the long building, which was the center of all the activity. A pair of hitching posts were practically filled, and he recognized the horses belonging to the Texans among them. Reining up, he was about to swing down when from within there blasted a six-shooter and a woman screamed.

5

Fargo knew better than to rush inside and possibly get himself shot to pieces. It was common knowledge that innocent bystanders were just as likely to be hit as those being shot at. Blundering into the middle of a gunfight invited a bullet in the brain. He slid to the ground and cautiously advanced to the open door.

There were close to thirty people inside. Eight were conspicuous as farmers due to their homespun clothes. There were three mountain men in beaded buckskins, the two Texans, and six women in dresses molded to their full figures. The rest were more of the same breed as Curry and Shanks, hard, cruel men who lived raw lives of violence, drink, and gambling.

The setup resembled a gambling hall more than it did a trading post, with fifteen tables on the left side and a bar on the right. Lying on his back beside one of the tables was a young farmer in a flannel shirt, his right hand clamped to a bleeding wound in his left shoulder. He was staring defiantly up at Shanks, who held a smoking revolver in his right hand.

No one paid attention to Skye. He saw the other farmers were in shock. The two Texans, standing at the bar, appeared disgusted. Near them was Curry, smirking in sadistic delight. The old trappers were watching the unfolding events alertly, each cradling a rifle.

"Now I'll finish the job," Shanks said to his victim and cocked his revolver.

"But he's unarmed," an elderly farmer protested.

"Then he shouldn't go around insulting other folks," Shanks said. His speech was noticeably slurred, his eyes bloodshot.

The farmer on the floor boldly sat up with an effort,

grimacing as blood seeped between his fingers. "What are you talking about? I didn't insult you, mister!" he said.

"Like hell you didn't," Shanks snapped. "I wanted you to drink with me, and you wouldn't."

"That's no reason to shoot a man!" the farmer exclaimed.

"Out here it is, sodbuster."

"But I don't drink," the farmer said.

Shanks pointed the gun at the young man's forehead. "Any last words for your friends here?"

Enough was enough. Skye Fargo had heard all he needed and he took a step forward, about to intervene and stop the farmer from being killed, when a grating bellow from the back of the room gave him pause. He spotted a bear of a man in a dark brown suit shoving through the customers.

"Shanks! Put that damn gun away!"

"This is personal, boss."

So this was Ben Killian, the big man himself? Fargo had to admit that Killian was impressive, a great hulk of a bruiser who looked as if he could bend saplings with his bare hands or wrestle bears to a standstill. Killian had a square, scarred face and hands the size of hams.

"Personal, is it?" Killian said angrily, storming up to Shanks who recoiled in fear even though he had his gun out and cocked and Killian's big hands were empty. "Since when do you have the right to pick quarrels on my time?"

"He thought he was too good to drink with me," Shanks protested, wagging his six-shooter at the farmer.

On the instant that the gun was no longer pointing in Killian's general direction, the huge man struck. His left hand snaked out, grasping Shanks by the wrist and twisting viciously as his right hand, balled into a gigantic fist, rammed into Shanks a few inches above the belt buckle. Shanks squealed in anguish, bending at the waist, and lost his gun when it slipped from his suddenly numb fingers.

"No, boss!" he cried.

Killian was implacable. He held onto the wrist and commenced slapping Shanks across the face. Again and again he savagely beat the helpless gunman, each blow rocking Shanks on his heels. Shanks unsuccessfully tried to ward off the first few blows, but after that he could barely stay upright, and if not for the firm hold on his wrist he would have fallen. His cheeks became flame red, and blood trickled from both corners of his mouth. His eyelids fluttered. It was then Killian let go at the same moment he planted a sweeping punch on Shanks's chin. Shanks flipped completely over and smacked onto the floor. He didn't move after that.

Fargo had seldom witnessed such a methodical pounding of another human being. One look at Killian's flushed, satisfied features was enough to confirm everything he had been told about the man. There could be no doubt Killian would make a formidable adversary.

The wounded farmer started to stand when Killian noticed and lent a hand. "Thank you, sir," the farmer said gratefully. "You saved my bacon. I know he would have killed me in another minute."

"I owe you an apology," Killian responded. "This should never have happened. It's my fault for keeping Shanks on when I knew he had a drinking problem." He glanced at one of the women who promptly came over. "Charlene here will take care of your wound. If there is anything else I can do for you, just let me know."

"You're very kind," the farmer said.

"I just don't want the members of your wagon train thinking they are unwelcome here. You're money is as good as the next man's."

The other farmers gathered around their wounded friend, and Killian moved to one side. "Curry, have two men put Shanks in his bunk. I want him kept there until I have a talk with him later."

"Yes, sir," Curry replied, motioning at a pair of gunmen. He started forward but halted in surprise when his gaze strayed to Fargo.

"What is it?" Ben Killian asked.

"The guy I was telling you about earlier."

Fargo abruptly found himself the sole object of attention for Killian and every one of Killian's men. He decided now was the time to take the bull by the horns and, hooking his thumbs in his gunbelt, walked up to Killian. They were both about the same height although

Killian was much stockier. "I rode over from Burke's to have a talk with you," he announced.

Killian, oddly, smiled. Some of his men, Curry included, began to ring them in, but he motioned them away. "My name, as you must know, is Ben Killian." He held out his right hand. "How about if I treat you to a drink and we can talk."

Perplexed, Fargo reached out. From all he had heard about the man, he'd half expected Killian to fly into a rage and try to pound him into the floor. Yet here the man was being as civil as could be. His palm touched Killian's, and they both squeezed. He could feel the raw power the man possessed and guessed that they were equally matched in the strength department.

It was Killian who broke the shake after glancing down at Skye's hand. He nodded at the bar and led the way over, skirting Curry and two men who were in the act of toting Shanks from the building. "If you hadn't come to see me, I was planning to pay you a visit," he commented as he leaned an elbow on the bar and snapped a finger at the bartender.

"You know about Carl?"

"When he didn't return from Burke's, I sent Curry and a few of my boys to fetch him. They brought back his body earlier. We've already planted it in a grave out back."

Fargo watched the bartender pour two whiskeys and bring them down the bar. He picked up his and took a sip. "Do you plan to try and even the score?"

"What the hell for?" Killian rejoined. "I'm told Carl and you had a few words. He had to back down, and Carl was never one to take that lightly." He paused to down half of his glass in a single gulp. "Curry rode into Burke's and Burke told him how Carl tried to kill you. So Carl had it coming."

Fargo set his glass on the bar. Burke had conveniently failed to mention Curry's second visit, which must have taken place while he was in the shack with Rosie. Once again it demonstrated how cozy Burke was with Killian's men and perhaps with the top man himself.

"I'm not a man who goes out of his way to hunt trouble," Killian was saying. "And there has been entirely too much of it at my place lately. If it keeps up I'll get

51

a bad reputation and lose all my customers. None of the settlers heading for Oregon will ever stop off."

Fargo merely listened. He remembered what Peterson had told him. Was it possible Ben Killian had a change of heart? Could a skunk change its stripes, or was there another reason Killian wanted to improve his reputation?

"I've given all of my men orders to go easy and not cause any problems with my customers or the few locals," Killian continued. "Carl didn't listen and paid the price. So did Shanks."

"What about Curry?" Fargo asked. "He was all set to gun down old man Peterson when I stepped in."

Killian swirled the whiskey in his glass. "That was different, I understand. Peterson called Curry a cheat, and you know there isn't a man worthy of the name who will let such an insult pass. Curry could have killed Peterson, and no one would have thought twice about it." He sighed. "I figure Peterson was still sore because he lost big here one night, and he took out his anger on Curry, which was downright stupid. But no one ever claimed that old coot was very smart. He hasn't been back in here since he lost, and I've heard he's been making wild accusations all the time. And anyone who spouts off at the mouth should expect it to catch up with him sooner or later."

"So there are no hard feelings between us?" Fargo inquired. He happened to gaze at the door as Curry reentered and took a seat at a table.

"Why should there be? Hell, I don't even know who you are."

"The name is Skye Fargo," Fargo disclosed and saw the other man stiffen for all of one second and then immediately recover his composure.

"Heard of you," Killian said. "I didn't know you were up in this neck of the woods. Are you passing through or fixing to stay awhile?"

"That depends," Fargo said and let it go at that. He didn't want any of Killian's crowd learning the reason he was in the region until it suited his purpose. If something had happened to Paul and Constance Moreland and their sons, there was an outside chance some of Killian's men might have been responsible. He polished off his drink and set down the glass. "Thanks for the firewater."

"Any time," Killian said. "And I'm glad there are no hard feelings between us. I'm a man who likes his peace and quiet. I hope we can be friends." He gave a polite nod, then walked over to Curry and leaned down to speak in a hushed tone. Curry glanced sharply at Fargo before the two of them headed for the rear of the trading post.

Fargo reasoned that it was only a matter of days at the most before every one of Killian's men and every mountain man within forty miles learned of his presence. No one, though, would guess what he was about unless Peterson discussed his interest in the Moreland wagon train. It was too bad Paul Moreland hadn't taken the advice of his father-in-law and joined up with a bigger train rather than head out with only four wagons. Such a small group was asking for trouble.

"Hey pard, come and join us!"

He turned at the familiar Texas twang and spotted Harkey and Lester at a table with a bottle resting between them. Harkey beckoned for him to go over so he did. As he crossed the room he noticed something peculiar.

There were fifteen tables used for playing cards or whatever scattered over half of the floor. And there weren't any two of them exactly alike. Every single one was different from the next. There were round tables, square tables, and rectangular tables. There were polished tables and simple unpainted tables. There were tables in excellent condition and tables bearing scores of nicks and gashes. There were high tables and low tables. Maple, oak, and pine tables. It was as if Killian had bought or taken in trade any kind of table he could find.

The chairs were the same way. As he took a seat he discovered his chair was completely different from Harkey's and Lester's. The chairs at the next table were likewise different. In fact there weren't more than two chairs of the same kind anywhere in the place.

"Didn't count on seein' you here," Harkey mentioned. "Did you see what that son of a bitch did to that farmer?"

"I came in on the tail end of it," Fargo replied. Near the far wall the wounded man was being taken care of

53

by the woman Killian had appointed to the task. The other farmers were gathered around him.

"It made my blood boil," Harkey said. "The hombre who had the stuffin' beat out of him was on the prod. I would have liked to beat some sense into his noggin my own self."

"Let's finish our bottle and get the hell out of here," Lester said.

Harkey hefted the whiskey. "At the price they wanted for this I aim to drink every last drop."

Fargo tipped his hat back. "You might have been better off doing your drinking at Burke's."

"We were fixin' to," Harkey said. "I was gettin' right fond of that Flo. But Burke went on and on about how much better this place is and how the women at Killian's put Flo to shame." He shook his head in disgust. "We weren't in the door five minutes and the farmer got shot. And these women ain't much to brag on."

The same thought had occurred to Skye. If he was any judge of character—and his lifetime on the frontier, where a man's life often depended on how well he took the measure of others, had made him shrewd in that regard—then the doves working for Ben Killian were the sort who had plied their trade far and wide and knew every trick in the book. They had a hard look about them even when they smiled.

"I figure we'll ride on to Oregon with the wagon train these farmers belong to. They leavin' the day after tomorrow," Harkey said. "I want to get up there and find a homestead of my own."

Fargo stared at the back of the establishment. He had seen Killian and Curry go through a door in the right-hand corner. The door was cracked open five or six inches, and as he looked he was surprised to see the face of a pretty young woman peer out. He could almost swear there was a hint of blatant fear on her features, but then she was roughly shoved aside by someone behind her, and the door slammed shut. Now what was that all about? he wondered.

"Care to buy a girl a drink, boys?"

One of the doves had materialized at their table. A red dress barely contained her plump figure, and her blonde hair had an orange tinge to it. Her fleshy lips pulled back to reveal small yellow teeth.

"Another time, ma'am," Harkey answered her.

"Yeah. We have somethin' important we're talking over," Lester chimed in.

The woman smirked and jiggled her bosom. "I can show you boys a time you'll never forget."

"Later maybe," Harkey said.

Disappointed, the woman strolled to the table where the three mountain men were seated.

"Lordy!" Harkey whispered. "Burke must need spectacles. Flo has every woman here beat all hollow. And Rosie was downright beautiful compared to this bunch."

"It's enough to drive a man to drink," Lester said and gulped the contents of his glass.

"Are you stayin' here long?" Harkey asked Skye.

"No," Fargo said. "I'll ride back to Burke's with you when you're ready to go." He stood and hitched at his belt, then spoke loud enough for those of Killian's men who were at nearby tables to overhear. "Right now I need to take a leak. Whiskey goes through me like water through a sieve."

No one displayed undue interest as he made for the door. Once outside he walked to the left corner of the building, spied a patch of bushes a dozen yards away, and strolled toward them while pretending to be undoing his pants. None of Killian's outfit followed him.

He stepped into the middle of the bushes and waited a minute to be safe. There wasn't a single person anywhere he could see. If the rest of the buildings were occupied there was no sign of the people inside. Ducking low and staying in the deepest shadows, he worked his way toward the end of the trading post where light framed a burlap bag that had been hung over a window as a crude curtain. He wasn't worried about the lookout, if there was one at so late an hour.

Fargo dropped to his hands and knees to crawl the final few yards. When he was directly under the window, he eased upward until he could glimpse the room within. Perched on a large chair behind a mahogany desk was Ben Killian. Curry leaned on the front of the desk, listening to him. Fargo didn't see the woman and concluded she must have left the office.

Then she appeared, stepping into sight on the left, an exceptionally attractive woman of twenty-five or so who wore a nice riding outfit typical of well-to-do women back East. Her slender hands were clasped at her waist. Red hair cascaded over her shoulders, a color admirably suited to her striking green eyes that now blazed with fury as she addressed Ben Killian.

Fargo couldn't hear all the words. Most were muffled because evidently she was speaking in a low tone. Still, he caught a few here and there. ". . . disgusting . . . no matter how long you . . . one day will be . . . deserve it." When she was done she sat down in a chair near the desk, her shoulders sagging, her lovely face a mask of sadness.

What did it all mean? Fargo mused. She looked so totally miserable he was strongly tempted to break in the window and demand to know what was going on. Doing so would ruin any hope of uncovering clues to the disappearance of the Morelands, not to mention being downright dumb. She didn't appear to be in any physical danger and might well be Killian's woman.

He ducked low when Killian stood. Moments later the light went out, and he rose in time to see the door close. Somewhere in that room was a safe, if Shanks hadn't lied to Rosie, and in that safe might be the answers he needed. Or some of them, anyway. He considered coming back another night with the proper tools and breaking the safe open.

A cool breeze was blowing out of the mouth of the rocky gorge, fanning the fringe on his buckskins. It also bore to his ears a faint yet distinct sound, the whinny of a horse.

Fargo twisted and stared up the inky gorge, his curiosity flaring. What would a horse be doing there? So far as he knew, there were no wild mustangs in the area, and most riders shied away from ravines and gorges in the dark. Did Killian keep horses back there for some reason? It was worth checking later.

A twig cracked underfoot at the front of the trading post.

Whirling and flattening, Skye spotted two men standing at the front corner. They were talking and neither seemed aware of him. Moving carefully he backed up until he could slip around to the rear, then he stood and stepped to the other end. A quick check showed the

56

coast was clear to the front, and he eased cautiously along the building to the corner, where he peeked out. Both men were still there, two of Killian's men smoking cigarettes. If he stepped into the open they would see him and might become suspicious.

He impatiently waited for them to finish their smokes and go inside. Most of the lights in the other buildings had been extinguished, and he took to speculating on what those buildings were used for. The cabins were probably for the hired gunmen and the house must be Killian's. There were lights on inside so he saw clearly when someone looked out a window. It was the same lovely woman again. Killian and she must have gone straight there from the office. She craned her neck, gazing wistfully at the stars until a hand fell on her shoulder and pulled her away.

Somehow he had to learn who she was and why she was with Killian. He thought of Rosie and decided to ask her in the morning. If anyone would know, she was the one. He heard low laughter and footsteps, and when he leaned out the two men were gone.

On stepping inside Fargo was surprised to see Harkey dancing with one of the painted women in unsteady rhythm to the tune of a slow song being played by a man with a guitar who was seated close to the bar. He walked to the table where Lester sat moodily contemplating a glass of whiskey. "I thought the two of you were all set to leave," he mentioned.

The corner of Lester's mouth curled upward. "We were. But Harkey polished off a third of that bottle in no time, and when that filly came over and batted her eyes at him he jumped up and started dancin'." He drummed his fingers on the table. "Looks like we'll be here a spell. You might as well head to Burke's without us."

Fargo didn't like the idea at all. If Killian knew the two were carrying all of their life's savings, which might amount to anywhere from a few hundred to a couple of thousand dollars, they would be in danger. He didn't believe Killian's statement about wanting only peace and quiet for one minute. "We could drag him out of here," he proposed.

"Not without a fight. When Harkey sets his mind to womanizing there's no changin' it," Lester said, watching his friend dance. "Might as well let him have his fun, and when he's done I'll take him to Burke's. Burke said we could sleep in the stable if we wanted." He gazed around the room. "I sure as hell don't want to stay here. Might wind up with my throat cut."

"I don't mind staying," Fargo said.

"We don't need anyone to hold our hand, thanks," Lester said a bit testily.

"Then I'll see you tomorrow," Fargo said and turned to go. If he tried pushing the matter it would only anger the Texans. They might be young, but they were as fiercely independent as the wild cattle that populated their part of the country.

He gazed past the bar at the shelves lining the wall and for the first time noticed the dozens of clean glasses and mugs on one of the higher shelves. Every single one was different from the next. There were tall ones, short ones, wide ones, and thin ones. There were ones made of clear glass and colored glass. And not a complete set in the whole bunch. They were just like the tables and the chairs.

Fargo's brow furrowed as he pondered the implications. He walked back outside, mounted the Ovaro, and rode off, passing Killian's house. All the lanterns within were out except one. As he went past he stared at the window in the hope of seeing the woman once more, but he had no such luck.

He twisted in the saddle to study the gorge but could distinguish few details. If he ran into Peterson again he intended to ask the mountain man about the surrounding country. There might be a way of getting into the gorge without having to pass the trading post and without being seen by the lookout Killian posted. If worse came to worst he could always climb down using a rope.

When the buildings were well to his rear he put his spurs to the Ovaro and headed for Burke's. If Rosie was still up he would pay her a visit and make certain Burke hadn't bothered either of the women while he was gone. Then he would hit the sack. Tomorrow promised to be a busy day, and if he should be caught at what he had in mind, it would be a day filled with gun smoke and flying lead.

6

The day started sooner than Fargo expected.

Dawn had just begun to tinge the eastern horizon with vivid hues of pink and orange when the thud of hoofs awakened him, and he opened his eyes and rolled onto his back. He had opted to sleep in the stable although Rosie had offered to share her bed with him, knowing full well if he took her up on her offer he wouldn't have slept a wink.

There was another reason he slept in a corner of the stable with his blankets spread out on a soft cushion of piled straw. Should Burke want revenge for the beating, he didn't want to risk having others caught in the cross fire. By closing the creaking stable door almost all the way and arranging piles of straw around the corner where he was to sleep so he couldn't be seen unless someone was right on top of him, he had made it extremely difficult for anyone to approach him undetected. And since the Ovaro made an excellent watchdog, he had slept without a care in the world, confident if Burke tried anything there would be one less son of a bitch in the world.

From the sound of things two horses had entered the stockade and halted in front of the stable.

Fargo sat up, threw off his blanket, and moved to the wide door in his stockinged feet, the Colt in his right hand. He rubbed his eyes before peeking out. What he saw prompted him to yank the door open and rush to the two horses.

Harkey sat astride his, his haggard features testimony to the amount of alcohol he had consumed the night before. He slumped in the saddle in abject despair, and when he turned to look down at Fargo his face had a haunted aspect. "It was my fault," he mumbled, choking on the words. "All my fault."

Lying facedown over the other horse was Lester, his arms and legs dangling, his wide-brimmed hat gone, his long hair matted with dried blood. His holster was empty, his six-shooter missing.

"What happened?" Fargo asked, appalled. He *knew* he should have stayed with them.

"I'm not rightly sure," Harkey said softly, releasing the reins to Lester's mount. "I drank a little too much and let one of those women talk me into paying a room in the back a visit. But I was having a hard time keepin' my eyes open, and I sort of passed out." He glanced at Lester and groaned. "Next thing I know, there's a lot of shoutin' and Lester is there tellin' this woman to give the money she stole back, and some of Killian's outfit come bustin' into the room. That there Curry started callin' Lester names and shovin' him and Les went for his gun."

"He never stood a prayer," Fargo concluded.

"No, sir. He sure didn't. Curry plugged him right between the eyes."

Fargo slid his Colt into its holster and stepped closer. Lifting Lester's head, he found a blood-rimmed hole less than half an inch above the nose. The exit hole in the back of the head was much larger.

"It was all my fault," Harkey said, gripping the saddle horn so he could lower himself to the ground. He tottered, still feeling the effects of his binge, then regained his self-control and walked around to stand beside his dead companion. "It's all my fault," he repeated morosely. "Les wanted to ride out of there and I wouldn't go."

"What happened after Curry shot him?"

"Someone hit me on the back of the head, and that's the last I recollect until I woke up with a terrible headache. I was lyin' in the dirt outside the trading post, and Lester was right next to me," Harkey revealed, putting a hand on Lester's shoulder. "They must have tossed us out the door."

"And your money?"

"Gone," Harkey answered forlornly. "All gone. Every last cent." He touched his midriff. "We were carryin' it in money belts we bought in San Antonio at one of them fancy-dress shops. Killian's bunch probably took them off us after Les was killed, while I was out cold." He scratched his chin. "I wonder how they knew we had it on us?"

Fargo could guess. Harkey had mentioned having money he'd saved up in the presence of Burke. If his hunch was right, Burke later informed Curry when the gunman paid a visit while retrieving Carl's body. Then Curry told Killian. He suspected that Burke persuaded the Texans to go to Killian's so they would be robbed.

"I think I'll sober up and go back there and kill Curry," Harkey declared.

"They'd shoot you dead before you got in the door," Fargo said. "I'm told there's always a lookout on the heights behind the post. He'd spot you coming."

"A lookout?" Harkey said, blinking dumbly. "Why would they need one of those?" He glanced at Lester's corpse. "Why, I reckon Killian and his outfit are nothin' but outlaws. They're killers and robbers, plain and simple."

"I think so too, but I don't have any proof," Fargo said.

"Those bastards shot my pard," Harkey declared. "I aim to pay them back." He angrily shook a fist, and the mere movement caused him to sway unsteadily. To stay on his feet he braced a hand against Lester's horse.

"Leave them to me," Fargo suggested.

"Are you a lawman?"

"No. But if I'm right, I'm not about to let Killian go on murdering innocent people. One way or another I'll stop him. Permanently."

"I'd like to help."

Fargo was all set to tell Harkey no, but the young Texan's tormented expression filled him with pity. He could understand how Harkey felt. If it had been a close friend of his, he would feel the same way. And perhaps, later, Harkey would come in handy. "I'll let you know. Right now we should bury Lester so you can get some shut-eye. You're no use to me in the condition you're in."

The Texan nodded. "All right. I won't raise a fuss 'cause right now I couldn't lick a rabbit with a club. But once I'm feelin' better I want in. And Curry is mine. You remember that."

Fargo nodded at the revolver on Harkey's right hip. "Are you any good with that six-shooter?"

"I'm not a gunman, if that's what you mean. But I can hit what I aim at."

"Well, we'll see," Fargo said and took it on himself to lower Lester off the horse. Together, with him doing most of the work, they carried the body out of the stockade and into a field to the south of the fort. Finding a soft patch of ground took some doing, and then Fargo returned to the stable to put on his boots and search for a shovel. He found one used to shovel horse manure, leaning against one wall, and took it back to the grave site.

Digging took the better part of an hour. Harkey insisted on chipping in, but he could barely keep the dirt on the shovel blade. He slowed them down terribly.

Fargo never complained. The profound guilt on the Texan's face told how important this was to him, so Fargo stood silently and waited his turn. When they had a hole four feet deep and several inches over six feet in length they gently lowered Lester into the ground. Harkey removed a few personal effects from Lester's pockets, then demanded that he be the first to drop dirt on top of the body.

The sun had cleared the horizon and was steadily climbing when they completed the job and strolled back into the stockade. The Texan appeared about ready to keel over from exhaustion and grief.

"You get some sleep," Fargo said, entering the stable first. He pointed at the straw. "I'll roll up my bedroll, and that spot is all yours."

"Much obliged," Harkey said weakly.

As Fargo knelt he speculated on whether the Texan would be safe there for the time being. He doubted Burke would do anything, and Killian wouldn't regard Harkey as much of a threat. They'd expect Harkey to sleep off the cheap liquor, then leave the country as fast as his horse could take him—which showed how much they knew about the new breed of Texans.

He brought in both horses and unsaddled them. As he draped Lester's saddle over the top of a stall he heard heavy snoring. Poor Harkey, fully clothed and flat on his back, was already deep asleep. He took a blanket from Harkey's bedroll and covered him, then tended to the Ovaro.

The sun was two hours high before he led the pinto outdoors and swung up. Smoke came from the chimney on the trading post, but there was no sign of life yet at the shack. The women must still be slumbering. As with most ladies in their profession they were accustomed to sleeping until practically noon.

He departed Fort Hall and cut to the northwest. In his mind's eye he had an approximate bearing on Killian's Trading Post and his real destination, the gorge. The land was suitably rugged, and occasionally he had to detour around a ravine or a hill to keep off the skyline. Twice he stopped to permit the pinto to drink and rest. Close to noon he swung to the south, and within forty-five minutes he drew rein in a cluster of stunted pine trees on the rim of a gorge that had to be the one situated behind Killian's Trading Post.

Skye slid from the saddle, tied the Ovaro to a low branch, and slipped the Sharps from its scabbard. Crouching, he crept to the edge and carefully lowered himself onto the bare earth. Because the gorge was at a higher elevation than the expanse of land stretching to the Snake River from the trading post, he got to admire a panoramic view of the entire countryside. To the north, east, and west it was desolate, a land seldom penetrated by Indians and even less frequently by white men. If Ben Killian had something to hide there wasn't a better hiding place anywhere.

The serpentine gorge appeared to be half a mile long and less than a quarter of a mile wide at its widest point. Sheer rock walls over two hundred feet high enclosed it from one end to the other with the exception of the opening near Killian's.

From Fargo's roost he could see a lot of barren ground and boulders on the bottom. Not so much as a bird stirred down there. He rose and jogged along the rim, staying a few yards away from the edge so he couldn't be seen from below. Of more concern was the lookout above the trading post. Would the man concentrate on the approach from the Oregon Trail, or would he also scour the whole gorge from time to time?

He reached a spot where the gorge slanted abruptly to the right, and knelt behind a boulder. Crawling forward, he stopped in surprise on discovering a spring, green grass, and a crude cabin. Even as he watched a herd of fourteen horses came around the next bend, some sixty yards away, and trotted up to the spring where they proceeded to quench their thirst. None wore bridles or saddles, yet none had that distinctive wild aspect so typical of free-roaming mustangs. They were tame horses. So they must belong to Killian.

Why were they kept in the gorge? Fargo asked himself and reasoned that it made sense because it would be easy to keep the stock penned in, and there was plenty of grass and water. The number of animals seemed unusual, though. What need did Killian have for so many?

He had to find a means to reach the bottom. Rising, he hiked farther along the rim, seeking a likely spot. After going almost forty yards he stopped and regarded a narrow cleft at his feet. It ran from the top to the gorge floor. If he were to press his back against one side and his feet against the other, he might be able to work his way down. But he would have to leave the Sharps behind. Reluctantly he placed the rifle under a flat, tilted rock where it would be safe from detection, and moved to the cleft.

As he eased into it he could see the hard ground far below and tried not to think of the grisly consequences should he slip. He braced his back and his legs as he had planned, then commenced a supremely cautious descent. Every move had to be methodical. First he lowered one leg a few inches, then shifted to lower the other one. All the time he had to keep his back straight, and he dare not relax the pressure or he might start to gain momentum and be unable to resist the unyielding pull of gravity.

Sweat soon caked his body. Repeatedly he wiped a hand across his brow to keep the perspiration out of his eyes. His back became sore and his muscles ached terribly. Since he had to crane his head forward to see the bottom, which reduced the pressure on his spine and increased the likelihood of slipping, he rarely bothered to see how close he was to his goal. He lost all track of time, and he was beginning to think he had made a grave mistake when at long last he could see the bottom clearly merely by twisting his head to the right. Shortly thereafter he came to the final dozen feet of cleft and found it widened considerably, so much so that he had to stretch his legs to their limit.

When Fargo judged he had six feet or less remaining he relaxed and let himself fall. Landing lightly on the balls of his feet, he crouched and drew the Colt, ready for trouble. The cleft wasn't far from the spring where the horses were now resting, and many of them had turned to face him. He stepped into the open, his back to the rock wall, and scanned the gorge in both directions. Other than the horses he was alone.

Before checking out the cabin he wanted to see what lay beyond the next bend. He quietly advanced until he could peer around the corner. There was more grass, a few boulders, and one additional feature he hadn't expected. Ages ago the lower portion of the left-hand wall had been washed out by a flash flood or had collapsed, leaving an enormous overhang, an opening twenty feet high and encompassing an acre in extent.

It wasn't so much the overhang as the objects under it that made Fargo whistle softly in amazement. There were eight wagons, all Conestogas, those massive prairie schooners favored by the settlers traveling from the eastern states to Oregon. They were all in excellent condition although most were covered with a fine layer of dust, evidence they had been there for weeks or months. Behind and beside and all around the wagons was an enormous collection of merchandise. There was furniture of every sort, mainly chests of drawers and a few tables and chairs but other kinds as well, including cupboards, stools, and even the frames of four-poster beds. There were crates and boxes and valises in abundance. There were piles upon piles of clothes. And on one side lay a mound of tools the height of a full-grown man.

Fargo was about to step around the corner and go inspect the articles when a whinny alerted him to a pair of riders heading up the gorge. He glimpsed a man and a woman, then drew back before they could see him, whirled, and ran to the cleft. Kneeling, he hugged the side. Unless they stared straight into the cleft he would be invisible.

He heard the thud of hoofs first, then a man humming. His thumb closed on the Colt's hammer when the riders appeared in front of him. The woman he recognized as being the same beauty he had seen the night before. The man, then, had to be one of Killian's riders, and it was the hombre with the walrus mustache he had encountered near the Snake River on the day he had arrived in the area. How interesting. It meant that whole bunch had been more of Killian's men.

They rode on past and up to the cabin.

Fargo inched forward so he could see them. The redhead dismounted and cast a baleful glance at Walrus.

"You've got no call to look at me like that, lady," Walrus said. "I ain't done you no harm."

"You work for Ben Killian," the woman responded and let the reins to her mount fall. "In my eyes that is more than enough to qualify you as the lowest sort of scum on this earth."

Walrus hooked a leg around his saddle horn. "You sure can talk fancy, ma'am. But you're way wide of the mark. Killian ain't such a bad sort."

"If you like vermin."

The gunman snorted. "Beats me what Ben sees in you. You'd as soon slit his throat as breathe."

"If I'm ever given the opportunity you can be assured I will," the redhead said. "Now why don't you run along and play with a Gila monster or something."

"There ain't no Gila monsters in these parts."

"Too bad," the woman said, moving to the door. She paused with her hand on the latch. "I was serious. Go away. Leave me alone, Toliver."

"I can't do that, Miss Lee, and you know it. My orders are to escort you up here so you can get some fresh air and stretch your legs. But I'm not to let you out of my sight unless it's when you're in the cabin."

Fargo had heard enough. He slid the Colt into his holster, then reached down and pulled the Arkansas toothpick from the slender sheath attached to his leg above the ankle. The situation called for stealth and silence. Any gunfire would draw Killian and company on the double. He stepped from concealment, glad Toliver's back was to him, and padded toward the gunman.

The redhead spotted him instantly. To her credit she only blinked once, then regained her composure and let go of the latch. Smiling sweetly, she strolled closer to Toliver. "Perhaps I am being unfair. Killian has stocked the cabin with everything I need. Why don't you come in and I'll fix you some coffee."

"Not on your life," Toliver said, shaking his head vigorously.

"Why not?"

"Killian would have me skinned alive."

Fargo knew she was deliberately distracting her guard so he could get close enough to use the knife. He had to admire her courage. Whoever she was, she despised Killian even more than he did and seemed to be a virtual prisoner. He was eager to learn her connection to the whole affair and counted on her shedding new light on Killian's activities.

"He'll never know," the woman told Toliver. She motioned for him to climb down. "Come on. What harm can one cup of coffee do?"

The gunman leaned over until their noses were almost touching. "I don't know what you're trying to pull, Nellie, but it won't work. Crossing Ben Killian is as bad as crossing a grizzly. And I intend to live a nice long time yet."

Skye was almost there. Ten feet separated him from the rump of Toliver's horse. He took each step with exquisite care, placing the soles of his feet down gently so as not to make any noise. The cushion of grass helped. He gripped the hilt of the toothpick firmly and tensed for the dash he was about to make.

"I'll talk to Ben. He'll understand," Nellie Lee said and made the mistake of glancing one more time at the big man in buckskins stalking the gunman.

Toliver turned. From the look on his face he wasn't expecting trouble, but that all changed the second he saw Fargo. "You!" he blurted and grabbed for his gun.

7

Fargo bounded forward, whipping his right arm back for an overhand throw, a technique he had practiced countless times. Nine times out of ten he hit the target dead center. But there was always that tenth time, always a chance of missing no matter how slight, and if he missed now the gunman would put two or three slugs into him before he could draw.

Toliver was fast, much better than average. His right hand began to sweep up and out, his Colt clenched securely and his thumb curling back the hammer. In another instant he would fire.

It was then that Nellie Lee unexpectedly leaped and grasped the top of Toliver's boot. She wrenched and heaved, jerking the boot out of the stirrup and lifting his leg as high as she could in a frantic attempt to unseat him and send him crashing to the ground. Startled and off balance, Toliver glanced down at her, momentarily taking his eyes off of Skye Fargo.

Which was all the opening Fargo needed. He hurled the toothpick with all the power in his shoulder and arm and saw the keen blade bite into Toliver's neck at the base of the throat. Toliver screeched and clutched at the hilt, forgetting all about trying to snap off a shot. And in two strides Skye was alongside the horse and taking hold of the same leg Nellie held. He shoved upward and succeeded where she had failed, upending Toliver and dumping the gunman on the grass.

Toliver rolled to his knees and yanked the knife free. He'd lost his revolver, and both of his hands were bathed in a crimson spray. "No!" he rasped out and tried to stanch the flow of blood by pressing a palm over the knife hole, but it was like trying to plug a ruptured dam with a cork. His lips moved soundlessly as he swayed, weakening rapidly. "You!" he finally screamed, jabbing a finger at Fargo. "You—!"

The redhead swiftly retrieved the discarded six-shooter and pointed it at the gunman's forehead. "We should finish him off," she said coldly.

"No," Fargo replied, grabbing the barrel before she could shoot. "The shot might carry all the way to the trading post. Do you want Killian to hear?"

"Oh," Nellie said. "Sorry."

He let go of the gun. Toliver sagged and had to support himself with a hand on the ground to stay on his knees. He looked up at Fargo, tried to clench his other hand into a fist and rise, but instead collapsed, sprawling onto his stomach with his arms outstretched. A few convulsions later he lay completely still.

"Good riddance," Nellie Lee said bitterly.

Fargo reclaimed the toothpick, wiped the blade on Toliver's pants, and replaced the knife in its sheath. Only then did he stand and study this hard woman he had evidently rescued from Killian's clutches. Up close her beauty was more obvious, more radiant. And he noted something else. Nellie Lee's eyes simmered with an inner fire that hinted at great strength of character. He instinctively liked her, liked her a lot, and it took a lot of self-control to keep him from openly admiring her physical charms as he addressed her. "The name is Skye Fargo. Am I right in thinking Ben Killian is holding you here against your will?"

"You are," Nellie answered. "He murdered my husband and stole all our belongings and then had the gall to propose marriage."

"Killian plans to marry you?" Fargo asked in astonishment.

Nellie nodded and scowled. "I'll see him in hell first. The man is a fiend. Not only that, I suspect he's insane."

Fargo gazed down the gorge. He wanted to ply her with questions, but paramount was getting both of them out of there before any more of Killian's band showed up. "Was Toliver the only one sent to watch over you?"

"Yes," Nellie said. "Killian didn't think more guards were needed. There's only the one way out of this gorge, and he has a lookout on top and two men in the entrance. I couldn't escape if I wanted to, and I certainly do."

"You can tell me all about it later," Skye told her. He squinted up at the rim, debating whether to try taking her up the cleft.

"How did you get here?" she inquired. "What's your connection to Ben Killian?"

"I'm the man who is going to stake him out on an ant hill and leave him for the buzzards," Fargo said. Could he use rope? There was a lariat on Toliver's horse, but it wasn't long enough to reach from the top of the gorge to the bottom. Even if he were to get his lariat off the Ovaro, combining the two wouldn't suffice. He wondered if there was additional rope under the overhang. "Is there any rope in the cabin?" he asked.

"No. Just a chair, a table, a stove, and some food. Killian wants me to be comfortable," Nellie said, spitting out the last word. "He won't let me out of his sight except for a couple of hours each day when I'm allowed to come up here to be by myself." She wagged the gun at Toliver. "Of course I always have one of his rabid dogs watching over me."

"How long does he let you stay here?"

"Until about an hour before sunset. He always tells his men to have me back at the trading post by dark."

"Come with me," Fargo said and made for the overhang. The horses at the spring had not been bothered by the commotion and were resting quietly. At the bend he stopped to scout the next stretch and found the way clear.

"Do you know where all this stuff comes from?" Nellie asked as they jogged toward the incredible collection of merchandise and wagons.

"I can guess," Skye replied. "Killian and his bunch have been robbing and killing settlers bound for Oregon. He has their wagons brought here, probably under cover of night, then takes everything he can use and stores the rest here to be sold later."

"That's a pretty good guess. Are you a lawman of some kind?"

"No. Folks call me the Trailsman."

"Never heard of you. What is a trailsman, exactly?"

"Where are you from?"

"New York City. Why?"

"I never would have known," Fargo said dryly while surveying the rim on both sides of the gorge. He detected no movement, saw no one up there. Farther down the gorge was yet another bend, the high wall hiding them from the lookout stationed near the entrance. They were safe for the time being.

"What is that supposed to mean?" Nellie asked.

"Remind me later and I'll explain," Fargo said. They ran under the overhang and he halted to study the piles of possessions. How many unsuspecting pilgrims must have been killed to provide such a haul? Twenty? Thirty? There were only eight wagons, but other wagons might have been chopped up or burnt or left deep in the brush. It was a cinch these eight hadn't carried everything stored here. He moved among the booty.

"Are you looking for something?" Nellie inquired.

"Rope."

"I'll help," she offered, joining in.

Fargo raised the lid on a crate and found a set of fine china inside. Some of the pieces were missing. He remembered all the different glasses and articles of furniture in the trading post, and his lips compressed in fury. Nellie Lee had been right. Men like Ben Killian were mad dogs who deserved to be exterminated. And he was just the man to do it. Not that he necessarily liked the idea of tangling with Killian's outlaw band, but there were no sheriffs or marshals or military outposts within hundreds of miles. And if Killian's outfit wasn't stopped then and there, scores of more lives might be lost since there was no telling how soon the bastard might strike again.

"Mr. Fargo?" Nellie Lee called out. She was standing at the back of one of the Conestoga wagons, peering inside.

Skye walked over. "Find some?"

Nellie turned, her lovely features contorted as if she was about to be sick. "No. Something else. See for yourself," she said and walked off on shaky legs.

Little wonder. Lying on the wagon bed in a jumbled heap were a dozen or more scalps, some fresh, some not so fresh, all with dried blood on the strips of skin to which the hair was attached. He reached in and examined one, the brunette locks of a woman, then tossed it back in disgust.

"Why?" Nellie said. "I knew he killed them, which is bad enough. But why commit this added atrocity?"

"He might be trading them with Indians," Fargo explained. "To a warrior a scalp is a mark of manhood, a symbol of bravery. But just like whites, not every Indian is as brave as he'd like to be. So sometimes a brave will trade for a scalp to hang in his lodge rather than go out and earn it the hard way. Doesn't happen often but it happens."

"I had no idea."

"It's not something any Indian likes to talk about. And no self-respecting warrior would do such a thing, so those who do don't brag on it," Fargo elaborated. He began hunting again and added, "It might just be that Killian likes to take scalps. Maybe he got into the habit awhile back and couldn't quit."

"How could anyone develop such a revolting habit?"

"From time to time there have been bounties offered on Indian scalps. Some men grow to like it."

Nellie Lee bowed her head. "Why I ever agreed to come out to this dreadful land I will never know."

"Your husband wanted to come?" Fargo asked as he checked behind a cupboard.

"Yes. Harry was tired of living in the city. He'd read all about the new land in Oregon and believed he could start over and become a successful farmer."

"What did he do for a living?" Fargo idly probed.

"He worked as a vice-president in a bank," Nellie said and quickly went on, "but he was born and raised on a farm so he knew all about farming. He always regretted leaving the country life to live in the city. Life there never did agree with him, and he desperately wanted to work with the soil again." She paused. "I was crazy to let him talk me into it."

Fargo saw a mound of discarded clothing to his right and went to investigate. He grinned when he saw a pile of coiled rope nearby. "Here is what we need," he announced. "Give me a hand." Nellie came over, and he filled her arms with as much rope as she could hold, then burdened his own arms to their limit. It was probably far more than they needed, but he would rather have too

72

much than too little, and he had no intention of coming back for more.

"I must sound like a terrible bore," Nellie said as they retraced their steps. "But you must understand. I like city life. I like the plays and the parks and shopping for my clothes instead of making them from scratch."

Fargo said nothing. The woman must have loved her husband very much to have given up the life she preferred for his. Harry had been just like the thousands of other discontented men back East who saw Oregon as a paradise and the answer to all their innermost dreams. "If you don't mind my asking, how long ago was your husband killed?"

"About two weeks ago. We were with a big wagon train, and we stopped because our wagon-boss saw Killian's sign and wanted to see about purchasing supplies. Mr. Jeffers didn't like Killian at all and didn't buy a thing. But Harry got to drinking, and the next thing I knew one of Killian's men rode over to tell me Harry was dead drunk. I took the wagon to get him, and that's when Killian first laid eyes on me," Nellie detailed, her voice lowering almost to a whisper by the time she stopped.

"You don't have to tell me if you don't want to," Fargo said.

"I need to tell someone, and I want you to understand. Killian offered to put us up in a cabin, and I didn't have any choice but to agree. Unknown to me he sent someone to inform Mr. Jeffers that we had decided to stay on for a while."

"Then what happened?"

"When Harry got over being sick we prepared to leave. But one of our wagon wheels broke as soon as we started out. Killian said he would have a man fix it. When two days went by and the wheel still hadn't been fixed, Harry went to talk to Killian. I was in the cabin, reading, when I heard the shots," Nellie said, and closed her eyes for a few seconds. "When I got to the trading post Harry was dead with four holes in his chest. Curry claimed Harry had picked a fight and gone for a pistol, but I know for a fact Harry owned only a rifle, and he had left it at the cabin."

Fargo saw the cleft ahead and slanted toward it. For

a woman who had been through sheer hell, Nellie Lee had held up well. He found his gaze straying to her ample bosom and her slim hips. And her face! She had to be one of the most beautiful women he'd ever met. It was no mystery why Ben Killian had taken a liking to her.

"I wanted my wagon fixed and someone to escort me to the Oregon Trail, but Killian wouldn't hear of it. I became his prisoner although he never actually bound me or locked me up. He said he was going to make me his wife and in time I would see things his way," Nellie mentioned, poison in her tone. "Like hell! I am going to see him dead if it's the last thing I ever do."

"I'll help you," Fargo responded. At the bottom of the cleft he dropped the rope, and she did the same. Kneeling, he began examining their collection, picking the stoutest lengths and knotting them securely.

Nellie peered upward. "You expect me to climb all the way up there?"

"I'll be helping you. We'll tie one end around your middle and I'll pull from on top."

"I don't know if I can do it," she said. "I've never been much for outdoor activities."

She stood only a few feet away, and when Fargo looked up he was staring at the junction of her shapely thighs as accented by her clinging dress. He mused on how she would be at indoor activities and shut the image from his mind. This was hardly the time or place. "We'll make it," he assured her.

She watched him knotting two ropes for a while. "You have lived in the West a long time, I take it?"

"All my life. I've made a few trips east now and then but I've never stayed long."

"Are there many men like Ben Killian?"

"There are men like him everywhere, men who take what they want when they want it and who don't give a damn about who they have to step on to get it."

Nellie shook her head. "You don't meet murdering butchers like him back East."

"No," Fargo said, testing the knot he had just made by tugging with all his might on the two ropes. "Back there you find cutthroats who use money and power and crooked lawyers to run roughshod over those who stand in their way. Out here the cutthroats use guns and knives. Different weapons, but it's the same thing."

"I never thought of it in quite that way," Nellie said, regarding him intently.

"If you want the truth, I'd rather have a man come at me with a gun than a lawyer. At least he's honest about it and not afraid to face you man-to-man."

"Have you faced many men with a gun?"

"Some would say more than my share," Fargo said, tying another pair of ropes together.

"Can you beat Curry?"

"I honestly don't know. They say he's very good."

"If need be you could shoot him in the back."

Fargo glanced up at her. "I'll pretend I didn't hear that."

"What's wrong? Curry killed my husband on Killian's orders. I want them both dead, and I think you're the man to do it. I saw the way you handled Toliver."

"I won't shoot a man in the back," Fargo said, rising. He stepped to the middle of the cleft and gazed skyward.

"What difference does it make?"

"To you, maybe none. But out here only cowards and bushwhackers go around shooting others in the back. A man has to meet his troubles head-on or he isn't much of a man. When it comes time to face Killian and Curry, I'll be standing in front of them, not behind them."

"Noble sentiments, but misplaced. Murderers like those two don't deserve fair play. You could be killed."

Fargo started wrapping an end of rope around his waist. He looped it three times before making a knot that would hold the rope in place until he reached the crest.

"You're as crazy as Killian," Nellie remarked.

"Killian might be a lot of things, but he's not crazy. He wants you, plain and simple, and he's willing to do whatever it takes to make you his. You should be thankful he hasn't just thrown you down on a bed·and gone at it."

"He wouldn't dare!"

"Don't put anything past him. I wouldn't rate Killian as the most patient man in the world," Fargo said, and held both arms out. His fingers didn't touch. "Do me a favor and bring your horse over."

Nellie looked overhead and grinned. "I doubt he can climb that high," she said and hastened to comply. She led the bay back and awaited further instructions.

"Hold him steady," Fargo directed, turning the horse so the saddle was directly under the cleft. Mounting, he eased first his right leg and then his left leg up until he could put both feet on the saddle and slowly stand. The bay shifted uncomfortably but stayed put. He was now high enough to brace his back against one side of the cleft and his feet against the other. "You can take the horse away," he said.

"Be careful," Nellie replied, leading the animal off a few yards.

"When I get to the top I'll wave," Fargo stated. "Tie the other end of the long rope I've made around your waist, climb on the bay, and wait until I start pulling. Hold fast and use your legs for support. You should do fine."

"I'll try."

Fargo smiled encouragement and climbed. Where the descent had been extremely difficult, the ascent was even worse. He had to exert constant pressure to resist the pull of gravity, his muscles aching from the start. As before he became covered with sweat. He settled into a routine of lifting a foot, shifting, and lifting the other. From his perch he could see the western horizon, and he was acutely aware of the sun as it slowly dipped lower and lower.

The strain became almost unbearable. He plodded ever higher, moving more on instinct than design. His shoulders throbbed. When he eventually felt a gust of wind hit his face and saw the rim almost within reach, he relaxed in relief, slipped, and would have plummeted to a gruesome death had he not jammed both boots into the opposite wall to arrest his slide.

Wiping his forehead on a sleeve, Fargo concentrated and covered the last couple of yards. He hooked his elbows over the rim, pushed with his legs, and scrambled out. For a minute he lay there, catching his breath. The sight of the sun hovering over the distant western horizon galvanized him into standing and untying the rope from around his waist. He toyed with the notion of going for the Ovaro but decided it would take too much precious time. Instead, he turned, secured the rope about a boulder, then moved to the edge and waved to Nellie Lee. Gripping the rope in both hands, he waited until she was on the horse and heaved.

At first he thought his arms would be wrenched from their sockets. But once she had her legs braced on the wall much of the strain vanished. Pulling hand over hand he raised her higher and higher. For someone who had implied she didn't get much exercise, she did remarkably well. Twice she called up to him and asked to rest for a bit. After each interval she climbed with increased vigor.

The sun had partially dipped from view when Fargo finally pulled her onto the rim. He released the rope to grab her under both arms and pulled her to safety, then sank down beside her and exhaled loudly. "You sure took your time," he joked.

"And you must be all muscle," Nellie said, her eyes roving over his powerful physique.

For a few moments they sat in awkward silence until Fargo thought of something to say merely to keep the conversation going. "How did a woman from New York City wind up with a name like Nellie?" he asked. "Don't girls back East usually have names like Mary and Susan and Elizabeth?"

"My maiden name is Nella Vanhorton. But I never did care for Nella and insisted everyone call me Nellie."

Fargo was about to compliment her decision when from the bottom of the gorge there arose an enraged shout.

8

Skye Fargo moved to the rim and risked a peek. Five riders had arrived at the cabin and one of them, Ben Killian, was examining Toliver's body. Even as he looked, Killian stood and motioned at the others who then fanned out to search for Nellie. Killian stalked toward the cabin.

"They'll be after us now," Nellie said. She had crept to his side and was glaring at Killian.

"If we're lucky, not for a while yet," Skye said. "Your horse has wandered over to the spring. Unless they find the rope we left at the bottom of the cleft, they'll figure you're somewhere in the gorge. By the time they search it from one end to the other we can be long gone." He backed away, retrieved the Sharps, and paused to scan the south end of the gorge. There was still no evidence of the lookout. The man must be positioned among boulders or some other sheltered nook where he couldn't be spotted. "Follow me," he said and led the way north.

He took only three strides when something struck a boulder to his right, causing rock slivers to fly in all directions, and a heartbeat later the crack of the shot rolled along the gorge and echoed off the high stone walls. Whirling and taking a step to the left, he spied a man with a rifle well over two hundred yards away, perched on a boulder on the opposite rim. It had to be the lookout, and the man must have spotted them when they came up out of the cleft and worked his way toward them for a clear shot.

"Get down!" Fargo barked, pressing the Sharps to his right shoulder. The lookout's rifle boomed again, and this time an angry hornet buzzed harmlessly past Fargo's head. He cocked the Sharps and held the barrel at just the right angle to allow for the range and the fact he was a hundred feet or so higher than the lookout. Yelling erupted down in the gorge, but he ignored it.

The lookout was also taking careful aim.

Fargo fired, the Sharps bucking against his shoulder, and saw the man throw his arms into the air and pitch from the boulder. The lookout struck the rim, voiced a plaintive scream, and toppled over the side. His arms and legs thrashed wildly until the very moment he thudded onto the rocks far below.

"You did it!" Nellie declared.

"We have to run," Fargo said, grabbing her arm and hauling her upright. "Let's go." He spun and sprinted northward. His plan to spirit the woman safely away before her absence was discovered had been ruined. Now it was a simple race to see how much distance he could put behind them before Killian's bunch could reach the north end of the gorge and begin tracking them. He estimated Killian would need ten minutes, at least, to gallop to the gorge entrance, round up extra men, and reach the north end.

A ten-minute head start wasn't much of a lead. He wished they had an extra horse. When they came to the pinto he swiftly jammed the Sharps into the saddle scabbard, then mounted and offered his hand to Nellie Lee. She took it and swung lithely up. "Hold on tight," he cautioned, and after she looped both arms around his waist and molded the front of her voluptuous body to his back he wheeled the Ovaro and headed to the northwest. There were two reasons. First, Killian might suspect he was the one who had rescued her and might figure he would head for Burke's, which lay to the northeast, and rush straight there. Second, there was dense forest to the northwest, and if Killian didn't act impetuously and ride off to Burke's without checking the tracks, he would stand a better chance of losing the gang in the forest than anywhere else.

The Ovaro galloped at a tireless pace, unaffected by having to carry two riders instead of one.

Fargo repeatedly glanced over his shoulder. Every time he did his face came within inches of Nellie's, and he could feel her warm, excited breath on his cheek.

It took considerable effort to concentrate on the gorge and not be distracted by her beauty.

"Any sign of them yet?" she asked when he looked back for the fourth time.

"No. I'd guess Killian is rounding up every man he has right about now."

"Please don't let them get their hands on me again. I don't know if I could take it."

"Seems to me you've done just fine so far."

"Only because my hate sustained me. I hate Ben Killian more than any person should ever hate another. I want to see him beaten, crushed, dead," Nellie said passionately, then her voice lowered. "But it was hard to be strong all the time. I kept having an impulse to curl up into a little ball and bawl my brains out."

"But you didn't. I suspect you're stronger than you think. Most people are."

"I wish I was as strong as you are. The way you stood there taking aim while that outlaw fired at you was the bravest thing I've ever seen."

Fargo shrugged. "I just did what I had to. Out here men and women learn to do what they must or they don't survive very long."

"I don't care to stay out here. With Harry dead all I want is to make it safely back to New York City, and I can guarantee I'll never leave the city again. I've learned my lesson."

Fargo rode a dozen yards before he commented, "Might be a shame to go on back when you're so close to Oregon. There's a real shortage of women out there and you could take your pick of just about any man you wanted. They'd be falling over themselves to court you."

Nellie sniffed. "I don't think I want to be a farmer's wife now. It would be too painful. I'd be reminded of Harry all the time."

"Oregon has more than farmers. There are merchants and miners and all sorts. In a few years some of the towns will be as big as most you find back East."

Nellie made no reply, and Skye goaded the Ovaro on until they were almost to the tree line. He shifted to check the gorge one final time and it was well he did. A large group of riders had appeared. They were almost to the spot where he had tied the pinto. He didn't know if they had spotted Nellie and him yet since they were shrouded in twilight. With a jab of his spurs he raced the stallion into the forest and threaded among the trunks and thickets.

For over an hour he rode hard, swinging in a gradual loop to the southwest. Where possible he stuck to the hardest, rockiest ground he could find. Darkness claimed the land when he emerged into a clearing and discovered a small pool of water at the base of a low cliff. "You can stretch your legs if you like," he told Nellie as he drew rein.

"Do you think we've lost them?" she asked, swinging to the ground with his assistance.

"I doubt it. Killian probably has a tracker or two in his outfit. They'll dog our trail for days."

"What can we do?"

Fargo dismounted and let the Ovaro drink. "I figure to cut the Oregon Trail. If we can find a big wagon train I'll leave you with them. Killian wouldn't dare tangle with a train of any size because he'd be too outnumbered and outgunned."

"Then what will you do?" Nellie inquired, idly arching her spine as she stretched. Her breasts swelled against her dress until even the nipples showed.

Fargo was suddenly thirsty himself. He knelt by the pool and removed his hat. "I'm going back to deal with Ben Killian." Leaning forward, he cupped a hand in the water and took a sip. "And I hope to earn my pay by finding out what happened to the Moreland family. They were last seen at Fort Hall by a drummer heading east. I suspect they went on to Killian's."

"Someone has hired you to find them?"

"Constance Moreland's father, Thomas Edgerton. He got all upset when he didn't hear from them as he should have, so he started asking around and advertising for information. It was sheer luck he came across the drummer. Then he had someone find me and hired me to track down the family."

"Moreland?" Nellie repeated, her forehead creased in thought. "No, I'm sorry, the name doesn't ring a bell. Neither Killian or any of his men ever mentioned the name."

"I doubt they would if they killed them," Fargo said.

"From what Edgerton told me, Moreland's wagon was loaded with fine belongings. And Moreland was well-to-do so he always carried a lot of money. Since he was traveling with just a few other wagons, he would have been easy prey. Killian would have done the same to Moreland as he did to you and your husband."

"Did they have children?"

"Two young boys."

"How horrible."

Fargo took another sip. "I don't have much to go on besides descriptions of the family and the fact Constance Moreland liked to wear red bonnets."

Nellie had been gazing at the sky. Suddenly she swung around sharply. "Red bonnets, you say?"

"Yeah. Why?"

"Because about two days after Killian murdered Harry he came to my room with a lot of gifts. Jewelry, clothes, and the like. And among the clothes were three red bonnets. I remember them distinctly because I thought it was strange he would have so many the same color."

"Damn," Fargo said softly, rising. It wasn't much, but it might be the only proof he would uncover unless Ben Killian or one of Killian's killers confessed, which wasn't very likely.

"Oh, Skye!" Nellie exclaimed, grasping the grisly implications. "But what could have happened to the boys? Surely not even Killian would go so far?"

"He wouldn't leave witnesses."

"But to murder children!" Nellie said, aghast, and then blinked as if in surprise. "The Indians! That must be the answer."

"What Indians?" Fargo asked, stepping over to her.

"I don't know which tribe, but I do remember overhearing a conversation between Killian and Curry. They were in the next room, talking about how some of their wagons had made it to California and how glad they were the Indians had agreed to give them safe passage."

Wagons to California? Fargo folded his arms across his chest and pondered. There might be more to Killian's operation than he had believed. The son of a bitch might be taking stolen goods down the California Trail to Sacramento or San Francisco and selling them, which meant the wagons would pass through Bannock, Paiute, and

Modoc territories, among others. Maybe, to ensure the Indians wouldn't bother him, Killian had worked out a trade of some sort.

"Curry also said something about handing over the three little ones," Nellie related. "At the time I didn't know what he meant. Do you think . . . ?" she asked and left the sentence unfinished.

"Could be," Fargo said. "Some Indian tribes never kill white women and children. They take them captive and raise them as members of the tribe."

"Oh, God," Nellie said.

Fargo walked to the pinto, debating whether to stop for the night or keep going. It would be best, he reasoned, to add to their lead so he stepped into the stirrups and beckoned for her to climb up.

"Are we riding all night?" she asked.

"Another hour or so should be enough. Then we'll bed down," Fargo responded, moving out. They soon reached a line of hills and he rode along their base until a shallow stream, barely a trickle of running water, prompted him to stop. He attended to the stallion while Nellie gathered wood for their small fire.

"I wasn't thinking," she remarked. "I should have brought some provisions from the cabin."

"We'll make do," Fargo said, opening his saddlebags to remove pieces of jerky. "It's not much but I'd waste my time trying to hunt in the dark."

Nellie turned to regard their back trail. "Do you think Killian will stop for the night too?"

"He can't very well track at night unless he uses torches," Fargo answered. "And he won't do that because he knows we might see them."

"What about our fire?"

Fargo had built it beside the stream and well below the low bank on the east side. As it was below ground level there was scant chance of anyone seeing it from afar and he told her as much.

"You think of everything," Nellie complimented him.

"I've had a lot of practice saving my scalp from war parties and outfoxing bastards like Killian," Fargo said. He spread his bedroll out between the fire and the bank and nodded at the blankets. "You can turn in whenever you want."

"What about you?"

"I'll sit up late to make damn sure we're not being trailed, then I'll get some shut-eye."

"You'll sleep on the ground?"

"I've done it before," Fargo told her. He chewed on his jerky and fed a few branches onto the fire. The flames crackled and hissed and he inhaled the acrid smoke.

Nellie sat down on the blankets. "I won't hear of it. There's room enough for both of us. I insist that you share your bedding with me or I'll sleep on the ground too."

"I toss and turn a lot sometimes," Skye warned her, grinning.

"So do I."

He got his canteen, filled it at the stream, then offered her a drink. They shared more jerky, and she talked about the long, arduous journey from New York to the Snake River region. Awe tinged her tone as she told of the enormous herds of buffalo she had seen and her first impressions of Indians based on her encounter with a family of peaceful Sioux at Fort Leavenworth. And when she told of her feelings on first beholding the majestic Rocky Mountains, her face and eyes seemed to light up with an inner glow.

Fargo nibbled on his jerky and let her gab, the fire warming his feet and legs. Here, in his opinion, was a city-bred girl who had learned to love the wide open spaces no matter what she said about not wanting to stay in the West. He made few comments, and before too long she had crawled under the top blanket, still chatting away about the dubious benefits of living in New York City.

"A person can walk down the street without having to worry about being attacked by Indians or outlaws or stepping on a rattlesnake," she said and suppressed a yawn. "And all the food you need can be bought at the store. You don't have to go out and shoot your supper and skin it before eating."

He saw her eyes close while she kept on talking, her voice becoming lower and lower until finally she stopped in the middle of a sentence and uttered a weary sigh. Moments later she was snoring lightly. He walked over, squatted, and pulled the blanket up to her chin.

Stars dotted the heavens. He picked up the Sharps and went along the bank until he was in total darkness. There he picked a spot on a patch of grass and made himself comfortable. In the distance a wolf howled and was answered by another. An owl hooted deep in the woods. All around the night sounds of the wild creatures told him that all was calm. Had there been a large body of horsemen in the vicinity he would have known from the lack of insect and animal noises.

To be on the safe side he stayed awake until close to midnight judging by the positions of the Big Dipper and a few other prominent constellations. Every frontiersman worth his salt learned to read the night sky, to estimate time and direction almost as accurately as with a watch or a compass. Since the tranquil night had not been disturbed, he rose and walked to the bedroll. Nellie lay on the right side, flat on her back, the blanket down around her waist again, her breasts rising and falling in rhythm to her heavy breathing. In repose her lovely features, accented by the soft golden glow from the crackling fire, were even more so. She was exquisitely beautiful.

He fed a few small twigs to the fire to keep it going for a while, then sat down on the left side of the bedroll, tugged off his boots, placed his hat and the Sharps next to the blankets, and laid on his side, his back to Nellie Lee. It was too bad, he reflected, she had recently lost her husband. She aroused him like few women, and he would have liked to get to know her intimately. But he couldn't bring himself to take advantage of her vulnerability. Sure, he liked women. But he wasn't the type to force or trick them into doing something they didn't want to do.

Thinking such thoughts, he fell asleep. He dreamed of the time he had spent among the Sioux some years ago, and of a particular Indian maiden who had shared his bed and lodge. The dream was so vivid that several times he believed he could feel the pressure of her lips on his, and once he was certain she was lying right beside him, her body tucked tight against his.

The chirping of gay sparrows greeting the new day awakened him, and instantly he became aware of pressure on his shoulder and a warm form snuggled in front of him. He had rolled over during the night and was now on his left side. Nellie must have also tossed and turned because she was sleeping so close to him her nose nearly touched his and her arm was draped over his shoulders. Her breath fanned his neck, and her breasts were within an inch of his chest.

He lay there, debating whether to get up and possibly awaken her, when she suddenly opened her eyes. She blinked, then realized they were lying face-to-face and instinctively drew back, withdrawing her arm.

"Oh, my! How did that happen?"

"People roll around in their sleep," Fargo said, sitting up. He yawned and stretched and gazed at the eastern horizon where the first rays of pink and reddish light heralded the advent of the new day.

"I was more on your side than you were on mine," Nellie commented. "I apologize for disturbing your sleep."

"You don't hear me complaining, do you?" Fargo responded. He shoved off the blanket, found his boots, and upended them to make sure a spider or a snake hadn't moved in during the night. Both were empty so he pulled them on and stood. "I'm afraid all we have for breakfast is more jerky and water."

"I don't mind. At least I'm no longer in Ben Killian's clutches," Nellie responded. Rising, she went off into the bushes and was gone a full ten minutes.

By then Fargo had the Ovaro saddled and was working on the bedroll. He looked up as she approached and marveled at how presentable she had made herself. Her dress had been wiped clean of dirt and bits of grass, her face and neck were freshly washed, and her hair was full and luxurious. If he lived to be a hundred he would never understand how women achieved such a remarkable transformation even in the middle of remote wilderness.

"I must be a mess," Nellie remarked self-consciously, smoothing her dress with her palms.

"I've known women who would give everything they own to be as good-looking as you are," Fargo replied. He finished rolling the bedroll and tied it with two strings, one near either end, then secured it on the pinto behind the saddle. After checking the Sharps he fed fuel to the glowing embers of their fire and soon had flames licking at the dry branches again.

"Will we reach the Oregon Trail today?" Nellie inquired while chewing on jerky.

"We should hit it this afternoon."

"What are the odds of finding a wagon train?"

"Depends. There are a lot of settlers heading west this time of year. Sometimes there are trains not more than a few miles apart."

"And at other times?"

"There might not be a wagon train by for days at a stretch," Fargo said, and added when she frowned, "If we're lucky the train that stopped near Killian's a couple of days ago won't be far down the trail."

They finished their meager breakfast in silence, and several times Fargo caught her studying him when she thought he wasn't paying attention. Not knowing what to make of it, he didn't bother to try. When the last bite of tangy jerked venison was in his mouth he doused the fire with water from the stream and dispersed most of the smoke by vigorously waving both hands through the thin column. Then he swung onto the stallion and offered his hand to her.

He rode due south, intending to strike the Oregon Trail as soon as possible. For hours the pinto covered the rugged terrain. He halted at midmorning to give the horse some rest and let Nellie drink from his canteen.

She swallowed gratefully, then asked an unexpected question that caught him by surprise. "Have you ever been married, Skye?"

"No."

"Ever plan to?"

Fargo shrugged. "Maybe one day. Who knows? But right now I'm happy with the way things are. I like to wander, Nellie, and it might be years before I get all the wandering out of my system."

"I figured as much," Nellie said rather sadly and extended the canteen.

He took it, and he could have sworn she deliberately pressed her hand against his and let the touch linger. She smiled enigmatically, pivoted, and strolled off, admiring the scenery. He watched her hips sway and wondered if she had in mind what he thought she had in mind. If so, why? He hadn't done anything to encourage her.

Onward they went. Fargo stopped only once more,

briefly. The sun had passed its zenith and was starting on its downward arc toward the west when he spied two thick spirals of smoke about at the point where he guessed the trail to be. "Do you see those?" he asked.

Nellie nodded, her chin brushing his shoulder with each bob of her head. "A wagon train, you think?"

"I'd say so," Fargo said and angled the Ovaro toward the smoke. "In half an hour you'll be safe."

"And I owe it all to you," Nellie said. "I'll never be able to repay your kindness."

"It's not necessary."

"I want you to know I've been thinking about what you said concerning Oregon. It doesn't sound like such a bad place. The wagon-boss even told us that the Indians up there are friendly."

"Most of them," Fargo said.

"Maybe I will stay there awhile and see what the country has to offer. I shouldn't judge it prematurely. Not after coming so far, not after all Harry went through to get us there. I'll decide whether to stay or not later."

Fargo was skirting a stand of dense trees north of the Oregon Trail. The fires creating the smoke were just on the other side. The familiar rutted track came into sight and he gazed to his left, seeking the Conestogas he was certain were there. Since he knew Ben Killian couldn't possibly have beaten him to the spot, he wasn't worried on that score. Not until he saw the seven men ringed around the two fires with their mounts nearby and recognized one of the men as the laconic gunman who had been with Toliver at the Snake River.

"Look!" that gunman now bellowed, rising and pointing at Fargo and Nellie. "Get them!"

9

Hauling on the reins, Fargo cut into the trees. Foliage closed around them as several shots split the air. Fortunately they all missed. He hunched low to pass under a limb and felt Nellie flatten against his back as she did likewise.

"It's some of Killian's bunch!" she exclaimed. "What will we do?"

"Keep quiet and hang on tight," Fargo cautioned, lightly jabbing his spurs into the pinto's flanks. Back on the trail men were shouting and horses whinnying as the outlaws scurried to get in the saddles and begin their pursuit. He was upset with himself for not checking first before venturing into the open. It made sense that Killian might have guessed he would try and take Nellie Lee to a wagon train and have sent some of his men along the Oregon Trail to head them off. When would he learn not to underestimate Ben Killian?

Once out of the stand he galloped to the northwest. Burdened as the Ovaro was Fargo couldn't hope to outrun the gunmen for long. He needed a place to make a stand, somewhere he could use the Sharps to its fullest advantage. A rise five hundred yards from the stand offered an ideal site. He goaded the pinto to go faster, and could feel Nellie's arm digging into his stomach as she held on for dear life.

Whoops and hollers told him the outlaws had burst from the trees, and a glance confirmed the band was fanning out. Five of them held revolvers while two had shucked their rifles. One of those snapped off a hasty shot that went wide.

"They're gaining!" Nellie declared.

And so they were. Their horses, all superb, hardy animals, were well rested and covered the ground rapidly.

Fargo knew they would catch him before he reached the rise. Something must be done to slow them down, and he had just the thing. Straightening, he yanked the Sharps out, drew rein so abruptly the pinto dug in its hoofs and slid several yards, and turned the Ovaro around. Three of the gunmen blasted away with their six-shooters, to no avail.

"Keep going!" Nellie urged him. "Don't stop yet!"

Paying no attention, Fargo aimed at the foremost rider who happened to be the outlaw from the Snake River. He sighted on the man's chest, the Sharps boomed, and a blink of the eye later the outlaw was flung bodily from his horse, as if by an invisible man. The rest promptly slowed or scattered to the right and left.

Bringing the Ovaro around, Fargo resumed his flight. He looked to the north, wondering where Killian and the majority of Killian's men were at that very moment. If they heard the gunshots they would be sure to investigate, and he would find himself partially hemmed in.

Although the hired killers fired frequently, Fargo reached the rise unscathed and halted. "Stay on," he shouted, sliding to the ground. As he fed another cartridge into the rifle he saw half of the onrushing riders slow down; they had guessed what he was up to. But a young outlaw in a brown hat and a red bandanna, a gleaming Colt in his right hand, recklessly raced straight at him, snapping off shots every fifteen or twenty yards. "Fool," Fargo muttered and aimed carefully.

The young rider tried to swerve, but as fleet as his horse was he couldn't hope to outrun a bullet. He twisted as the slug ripped into his torso high in the chest, then sagged with both hands on the saddle horn as he desperately tried to stay on his steed. But he went only ten yards before his hands slipped off and he tumbled to the ground where he rolled over several times and was still.

Fargo reloaded, tracked a second outlaw, and squeezed off the shot. A spot of crimson blossomed on the man's face and down he crashed. With three of their number dead the others didn't want any part of him. They reversed direction, making for the shelter of the stand as fast as their mounts would carry them, and he let them go.

In a bound he was at the pinto and climbing up, squeezing onto the saddle in front of Nellie. He inadvertently rubbed her with his leg from her shoulder to her hip as he did, and she blushed faintly. Beyond the rise lay more rugged land characterized by hills and gullies and strips of forest. Toward this he sped, hoping the rise would prevent the outlaws from discovering he had ridden off until he was well out of rifle range.

If anything, Nellie clung to him tighter than ever before, her breath warm on his neck. It annoyed him that he could be thinking of her lush body at such a time, and he forced himself to devote his entire attention to eluding Killian's men. He was worried about the amount of daylight left although he said nothing to her. More daylight meant the outlaws had more time to track him, more time to overtake him, before dark set in. And with the pinto bearing double there was no chance of outrunning the bastards. He must rely on his cunning and be like a fox leading a pack of bumbling hounds.

A gully appeared and he advanced along it for thirty yards before going up and over the side. Lady Luck smiled on him. For five or more acres the ground was packed hard and covered with rocks. Tracking would be exceptionally hard. He rode straight for half the way, then swung to the left for fifteen feet before changing direction yet again and riding due north. Four more times he practiced the same ploy. At last he rode clear of the rocky ground and into more forest.

The shade was cool and comforting after the glaring heat of the open ground. He patted the stallion's neck, his palm becoming slick with sweat. The pinto needed water and he had no idea if there was any within miles of their location.

Another hour was passed in swift riding. He surveyed the land behind them constantly and was gratified when the outlaws failed to appear. Nellie was resting her cheek on his shoulder, her breasts mashing into his back. Not once had she complained about the ordeal, as many women from back East would have done.

The sun climbed higher. As he rode he wrestled with the dilemma of how to get Nellie to safety. He couldn't simply leave her somewhere and ride back to deal with Killian. If something happened to him, she would be left stranded and helpless. But what could he do? If he tried swinging back to the Oregon Trail, there might be more of the gang waiting for them. Heading for Fort Hall was also out of the question. Killian himself and some of his men were somewhere between the region through which Fargo now rode and the fort. Besides that, he didn't trust Burke as far as he could heave a bull buffalo.

So what was left?

Maybe he should cut directly overland to a point well beyond where Killian's riders were likely to go and intersect the Oregon Trail there. With luck he might even overtake the pilgrims who had stopped recently at the trading post.

Skye peered up at the blazing yellow orb dominating the heavens, estimating the time remaining until sunset. They would have to spend another night in hiding so he must find a suitable spot.

"You say you've been to Oregon before?" Nellie broke their long silence.

"Yep. Pretty country."

"Know any of the women living out there?"

"A few," Fargo answered. He figured there was no need to tell her just *how* well he knew some of those women.

"Are they happy living so far from civilization? I mean, really happy?"

"I never bothered to ask them, but I'd say so. It isn't so much where a person lives as what they make of where it is that counts."

"You're an unusual man, Skye Fargo. Looking at you, one would never suspect that you're such a deep thinker."

Fargo couldn't help but laugh. "I don't know about that," he responded. "I've just been around. And when a man travels a lot he picks up a few things here and there."

"Scoff if you wish, but I know I'm right."

Amused at the notion, Fargo rode into a verdant winding valley, heading to the northwest. Soon he came to a wide stream and stuck to the bank. A sea of pine trees stretched into the distance on both sides. Lush grass bordered the stream. He saw signs of plenty of game and once spied a herd of mule deer in a clearing to the north. They raised their heads and watched him without the slightest trace of fear, indicating few white men had ever intruded into their secluded area. Normally it didn't take animals long to learn that man was a natural-born killer, the very worst predator alive, and to flee at the mere sight of a human being.

When the sun was poised to dip below the horizon he finally chose to stop beside a beaver pond. He gave Nellie a hand down, then slid off and took the pinto to drink. Without being told Nellie made herself useful by collecting wood for their fire. He stripped off his saddle and bedroll, stood back while the stallion rolled a few times, then pounded a picket pin into the ground near the pond so the Ovaro could drink in the middle of the night if it desired.

Fargo built a bigger fire this time, feeling confident their pursuers were too far behind to spot it. When the orange flames were leaping upward he rose and grabbed the Sharps. "I'm tired of jerky. How would you like some fresh meat for supper?"

"Is it safe? Firing a gun, I mean?"

"I doubt they'll hear it, and even if they do they're probably so far off they won't be able to tell which direction it came from," Skye answered and went to walk off when he noticed the apprehension in her eyes. "Here," he said, drawing his Colt. "Hold onto this while I'm gone. You never know when a bear or a mountain lion might wander on by."

Nellie gingerly took the heavy gun in both hands. "I've never fired one of these before."

"It's easy," Fargo said. "Use your thumb to pull back the hammer and squeeze the trigger when you're ready to shoot. Squeeze it, don't jerk it, or the barrel will tilt up and you'll miss."

"I'll manage," Nellie assured him and added, "but don't be gone too long, okay?"

Fargo nodded and hiked into the trees. Twilight lent the forest a gloomy gray aspect, but he could see well enough to distinguish details and came on a well-used animal run within five minutes. Small game used the trail to go to the stream. And while he would much rather eat venison, even if he shot a small deer there would be too much meat for Nellie and him to finish at one sitting, and he wouldn't be able to dry the meat or take any with him. So rather than needlessly kill a big animal, he planned to bag something that wouldn't go to waste.

Within ten minutes an accommodating rabbit hopped along the run on its nightly rounds. Concealed motionless behind a tree trunk a dozen yards off, Fargo aimed at its head and cocked the rifle. He had to be careful not to put a slug through the rabbit's body or there wouldn't be enough meat left to make a decent meal. At the click of the hammer the rabbit froze, its long ears erect to catch any more alien sounds, its nose twitching crazily in an attempt to detect the scent of any enemies. But Fargo was downwind and not worried. He took his time, then fired.

At the blast of the Sharps the rabbit leaped a full three feet into the air, spun, and crashed down on its back, its legs twitching convulsively.

Fargo moved from concealment and walked to the path. A second shot was unnecessary. The Sharps had all but taken off the rabbit's head. He grabbed hold of the rabbit's rear legs, dangled it in the air to let the blood and brains finish draining out, and retraced his route to the camp site.

Nellie was kneeling by the fire, the Colt resting in her lap. She beamed as he appeared and came out to meet him. "I heard the shot."

He lifted the rabbit into view. "If I had a pot I'd make some stew. How will roast leg of rabbit do?"

"My tummy is growling at the mere thought," Nellie said with a grin. "You let me do the skinning. It's the least I can do."

"You know how?"

"Harry used to take me hunting with him from time to time. Claimed a city girl like me should learn how to live off the land and make do for herself," Nellie replied and scrunched up her nose. "I never did like butchering an animal, but I know how."

"Have at it," Fargo said, exchanging the rabbit for his Colt.

"I'll need a knife."

He gave her the Arkansas toothpick, then sat down between the fire and the stream and reloaded the Sharps.

A few stars were out, sparkling brightly, and a cool breeze blew from the northwest, occasionally rustling the pines. He watched her work, suppressing a grin when blood splattered onto her hand and she shuddered slightly. Despite her abhorrence of the task she did a good job and removed the inedible portions quickly, although she scrunched up her nose when she gutted the rabbit and removed the entrails and organs except for the heart and the liver.

"Harry always liked rabbit hearts," she mentioned.

"You must have him on your mind a lot," Fargo said out of sympathy for her loss.

"I was trying not to think of him so much," Nellie said. "It was too painful." She glanced up, sadness touching her eyes. "Then you came along."

"What did I do?" Fargo asked in surprise.

"You remind me of him."

"Did he look like me?"

"No."

"Act like me?"

"Not exactly."

"Then how the blazes do I remind you of him?" Fargo inquired, perplexed. He thought he noticed her eyes glistening, as if with moisture, and wondered if she was about to cry.

"You just do," was all Nellie would say before devoting her attention to spearing large chunks of rabbit meat onto a makeshift spit.

Fargo prudently let the matter drop. He didn't want to stir up bad memories for her, memories better left alone, and he certainly didn't want a bawling female on his hands. So he sat quietly as the flames licked at the meat and a delicious aroma tantalized his nostrils. His stomach gave off a growl that would have done justice to a wolverine, and Nellie looked at him and laughed.

"You too?"

"Tomorrow I'll shoot an elk," he joked.

When the rabbit was done they dug in with gusto, eating as if a morsel of food hadn't touched their lips in weeks, ravenous for the meat. Nellie's fingers and chin became slick and shiny with grease but she ate on regardless.

Fargo had eaten his fair share and was licking the tips

of his fingers clean when a tremendous crash sounded in the nearby woods and something vented a rasping grunt. Before he could comment, Nellie dropped the small piece of rabbit she was holding up to her mouth and practically leaped into his lap, her arms wrapping around his neck as she clung to him in presumed fright.

"What is that!" she exclaimed.

"A bear would be my guess," Fargo answered while listening to the crash of underbrush as the bruin beat a hasty retreat. "Black bear, probably, coming for a drink when it caught our scent."

"Oh," Nellie said sheepishly, turning to face him. "Is that all?"

Suddenly they were nose to nose and almost mouth to mouth. Fargo could feel her right breast touching his chest and inhaled the scent of her hair and skin. His manhood stirred. He would have embraced her and planted a kiss on her delectable lips if not for the fact she had so recently been made a widow. To his amazement, she took the initiative and lightly touched her mouth to his, then drew back as if she had been shocked by a bolt of lightning and jumped to her feet.

"Sorry," Nellie mumbled.

"Don't be," Fargo said. "I liked it."

She spun, moved to the other side of the fire, and took a seat. Her features were downcast, her shoulders slumped.

"Are you all right?" Fargo asked.

"Fine," Nellie responded bitterly. "Just fine."

More puzzled than before, Fargo covered his confusion by drinking from his canteen. Her turmoil was all her own doing since he had behaved like a perfect gentleman so far. He figured she was attracted to him but felt guilty because her husband had been dead only a short while and now her conscience was warring with her passion. It was a personal matter she must resolve on her own.

He got up and went to the Ovaro. The pinto greeted him with a wet muzzle on the cheek, and he rubbed its neck and behind its ears, then gave it a rubdown using handfuls of grass. Spending time with his horse had become second nature. Since his life often depended on the stallion's performance he treated the horse as his best friend. Every man who rode the high country or the open range knew the value of a good horse, which was half the reason that anyone accused of horse stealing invariably qualified as the guest of honor at a necktie party. The other half had to do with the fact that a man left afoot in wild country was at greater risk of dying from thirst or hunger or being slain by hostile Indians.

When he returned to the fire he found Nellie already spreading out his ground sheet and blankets. "Planning on turning in early?" he asked.

"It's been a long day and tomorrow promises to be just as trying," she answered without looking at him.

He picked up the Sharps and made a circuit of the firelight, probing the darkness for signs of danger. For as far as he could see there existed only the night and the forest. If Killian's men were out there somewhere, they either had built their fire in a sheltered nook or else had made a cold camp. Something made a loud splash in the pond and he suspected it was a beaver. They were primarily nocturnal, most active in the early evening and shortly after dark. Satisfied all was well, he stepped to the fire.

Nellie lay on her side facing the blaze, covered up to her ear by a blanket. Her radiant mane of hair was the only part of her visible.

Sighing, Fargo again sat down and nibbled on a remaining piece of rabbit. The long hours in the saddle had fatigued him, and he had no intention of staying awake until midnight. Less than an hour went by before he moved to the edge of the bedding and set the rifle down. Once more he pulled off his boots, placed his hat to one side, and sank gratefully onto his back. He was careful not to touch Nellie. In her current mood she might haul off and slap him at the least little provocation. As he often liked to do, he gazed up at the celestial spectacle until his lids became heavy and he drifted into dreamland.

How long he slept he had no idea, but he was roused from his slumber by a moist sensation on his neck and chin. His mind responded sluggishly and he couldn't seem to organize his thoughts. For a minute he actually believed the Ovaro had pulled out the picket pin and ambled over to lick his face like an oversized dog, and then he realized how ridiculous the idea was and came fully awake with a start because the sensation was indeed being caused by a pair of lips, but human lips, not those of a horse.

Fargo opened his eyes. Nellie was beside him, her body pressed against his arm, nibbling lightly on his jaw. Her right hand rested on his chest and her foot touched his leg. "Nellie?" he said.

She raised up on an elbow to stare at him, a virtual goddess in the golden glow from the fire. "Don't talk," she said huskily.

He went to ask her if she was sure but she put a palm over his mouth to prevent him from speaking, then replaced the palm with her lips. Instinctively he darted his tongue out and was met by hers. She tasted delightfully sweet. Her silken tongue intertwined with his, then roamed over his gums and teeth.

Skye rose onto his side to face her, his lips touching hers the whole time, and cupped a full breast with his skilled fingers. He squeezed softly, then tweaked the nipple a few times, feeling it harden and become stiff yet tender. Nellie moaned low in her throat, her hand sliding down his front to grope his manhood through his pants.

Lust seized him as her fingers closed on his erect pole. He cupped the other breast and she squirmed in ecstasy. The breeze, which had been so cool before, didn't bother him at all as his body temperature competed with the fire to see which would cast off the most heat. His manhood strained against his leggings, demanding release.

In a deft motion Fargo rolled Nellie onto her back and shifted his left hand from her upper mound to her lower. She gasped, shivered, and kissed him more forcefully. Through the fabric of her dress he could feel the carnal heat of her slit and he stroked her vigorously.

"Oh, yes!" Nellie cried, digging her fingernails into his broad shoulders.

Skye caressed her inner thighs from her knees to her moist nether lips, intentionally fanning her lust slowly so that when he entered her she would be mad with passion. When she tried to press her legs together and trap his hand at the entrance to her womanhood, he yanked her dress up above her waist and slid his finger under her underthings. His forefinger brushed her core, and she arched her spine.

"I want you, Skye! I want you."

Not yet, Fargo reflected. Exercising delicate care he slid his middle finger into her hole and felt her wet inner walls close around it. Her smooth buttocks came off the blanket and ground into his callused hand, as if she would drive his finger all the way up inside of her. She panted heavily in his ear and clutched him fiercely. He lowered his lips to her right breast to suck on the erect nipple while his thumb crinkled her pubic hair and his forefinger plunged repeatedly into her innermost recesses.

"AAAAaaaahhhhh!" Nellie exclaimed. "I'm almost there!"

Her hips bucked furiously, and it was all Skye could do to keep his finger inside of her. He licked and kissed her left breast, then bent to kiss her flat stomach and insert his hot tongue into her navel. She was like a bucking mare, almost impossible to keep a grip on, but keep a grip he did, the friction on his finger building and building until suddenly she gushed within.

"Oh! Oh! Oh! Oh!"

He could feel her coming, feel the contractions that swept her beyond the brink of self-control. Her head thrashed wildly, her lips were parted in a red oval, and her breasts bounced as she humped up and down. His finger and hand were soaked, as were her thighs. He let her give free reign to her passion, and when at length she ceased cooing and wiggling and shuddering he reached down to release his rigid pole and lowered his knees between her legs. She looked at him, a satisfied smile curling her sensual lips.

"That was wonderful."

"I'm just getting warmed up," Fargo told her and buried his manhood inside of her. Nellie screeched, then bit him on the shoulder. Her vibrant body pulsed with desire. It was as if he had unleashed a tigress too long contained in a cage framed by her own conscience, and now that she was loose she was going to eat him alive.

Over the next two hours she nearly did.

10

A rosy arch of sunlight rimmed the eastern horizon when Skye Fargo awakened. Nellie was nestled against his left shoulder, and for a while he lay there thinking about their ardent lovemaking of the night before. When they had finally collapsed he had been exhausted. He still felt that pleasant lethargy a man often experiences after coupling with a woman, and he closed his eyes to savor it.

The distinctive metallic click of a revolver hammer being drawn back shattered the tranquility.

Fargo opened his eyes again and glanced to the right. Not six feet away squatted an Indian, a Bannock warrior in buckskin leggings and moccasins. Slung over his back was a bow and quiver. In his right hand was a brand-new Colt. His features were impassive as he motioned with the revolver, indicating Fargo should stand.

Moving slowly so as not to give the warrior an excuse to shoot, Fargo eased out from under Nellie and rose. He wore his pants but nothing more. His Colt and the Sharps were both on the edge of the blanket, and during the height of his lovemaking with Nellie he'd removed the Arkansas toothpick and dropped it into a boot. Now he was unarmed, at the Bannock's mercy unless he could lure the brave close enough to jump him.

Again the warrior motioned, directing Fargo to step away from the blankets, away from the weapons.

Fargo reluctantly complied. He was annoyed at himself for being taken by surprise. Usually his sharp senses would bring him out of a heavy sleep at the faintest sound. But last night he'd been exceptionally tired so his sleep had been deeper than usual. And, too, Indian braves knew how to move much more quietly than most white men. This one must have crept up before dawn, using the cover of darkness to hide him from the Ovaro, and then waited for Fargo to wake up. Clever. Real clever. But why? What did the buck want? At the moment the Bannocks were supposed to be at peace with the whites although the tribe had attacked wagon trains and trappers in the past.

The warrior stood and backed up several yards, then pointed his revolver at the ground and banged off three swift shots. The echoes rolled down the valley, startling a flock of birds into frantically flapping away from the pines.

At the first report Nellie sat bolt upright and looked around in confusion. She saw the Indian and recoiled in fear, then got a hold on herself. Lifting the blanket up to her chin, she hurriedly made herself presentable.

Displaying no emotion, the Bannock trained his pistol on Fargo but made no other moves.

Fargo scanned the valley. Those three shots had been a signal, of that he was certain, and a minute later his hunch was proven right when a group of riders appeared about half a mile off. They galloped toward the camp. Sitting tall in the saddle in the lead was none other than Ben Killian. Beside the huge man rode Curry.

So that was it, Fargo realized. Killian must be on friendly terms with the Bannocks, perhaps supplying them with some of his spoils or with captured women and children in exchange for safe passage through their territory and help when he needed it. He glanced at his guns, considering a mad dash to grab one to try and cut down the warrior before the outlaws arrived. Once Killian and his bunch got there, he would be hopelessly outnumbered and virtually helpless.

The Bannock saw the eye movement and took a step closer, a suggestion of a grin touching his mouth.

Fargo knew the man was just waiting for him to try something. He wouldn't take three steps and the buck would shoot him dead. Frustrated, he stood and watched the outlaws approach. Killian was smirking, enjoying his victory.

"Skye, isn't there anything we can do?" Nellie asked anxiously.

"Afraid not."

"I'll make a run for it. Maybe the Indian will come after me and you can escape."

"Don't be foolish. He'll put a bullet in you before you can get ten feet," Fargo said.

"I'd rather be dead than in that bastard's hands again," Nellie declared, standing.

The brave shifted the gun to cover her. "No try," he said sternly in heavily accented English. "Shoot in leg."

Fargo was ready to recklessly charge the Bannock if Nellie should try to make a run for it, but she froze when the Indian addressed her. He could hear the pounding of many hoofs yet didn't bother to look at the gang. He was more interested in the warrior. "Nice gun you have there. Where did you get it?"

"Killian give."

"I bet he's given your people a lot of things lately," Fargo said.

"Killian good man," the Bannock replied.

"Has he given you any women and children?"

The brave raised the Colt and pointed it at Skye's head. "Talk too much, white man. Mouth shut or die."

Fargo didn't press the issue. He had the answer he needed. Resigned to the inevitable, he turned, facing the riders. Ben Killian's smirk had evaporated and he was scowling. "Howdy, Ben," Fargo greeted him. "Why don't you make yourself comfortable, and I'll see if I can rustle up some leftover rabbit for breakfast?"

Killian disregarded the sarcasm. He was staring intently at Nellie, clearly angry. When only a dozen steps off he reined up and jumped down. "What the hell is the meaning of this?" he demanded of her. "Did the two of you share the same bed?"

"That's hardly a question a gentleman asks a lady," Fargo said, trying to divert attention away from her. He succeeded beyond all expectations as Killian marched right up to him and slugged him in the stomach.

"You'll speak when spoken to, you son of a bitch."

Fargo was doubled over, his stomach aflame with pain, trying to catch a breath. He tottered backward, giving himself a little room to maneuver should Killian come at him again.

"Leave him alone!" Nellie Lee stated, striding over to them, her fists clenched. "I wish I was a man, Ben Killian, so I could pay you back in kind for your violent ways, for murdering my husband and causing so many decent people so much misery."

"Curry killed your husband, not me," Killian replied lamely, his gaze on the blankets.

"Do you think I'm a fool?" Nellie snapped. "Do you think I don't know it was you who gave the order? Do you think I don't know that you're a disgusting, filthy, de—"

Killian hit her, an open-handed slap across the cheek that rocked Nellie on her heels. Seizing her by the shoulders, he shook her so hard her teeth chattered, then flung her to the earth. "You keep your mouth shut, whore, or I'll have the Bannock peel your skin off and chop you into little pieces." He jabbed a blunt finger at the bed-roll. "I've got eyes, bitch. You and Fargo slept together, didn't you? You made love to him, but you never would to me!"

Fargo was breathing normally. He saw Nellie flush with fury and knew that she was about to say something that would enrage Killian even more. He went to speak first, to cut her off, but she retorted before he could.

"I'll never go to bed with you of my own free will! You're contemptible! I hate you as I've never hated anyone or anything. And if it's the last thing I ever do, I swear I'll make you pay for having my husband killed. You filthy pig!"

Bending down, Killian grabbed her by the front of her dress and yanked her upright. His massive right fist drew back to strike her when he paused, his lips twitching from his rampant wrath. "No," he growled and shoved, causing her to trip and fall to one knee. "This is what I get for trying to do right by you, for being so damned stupid. I should have taken what I wanted like I've done with every other woman. But I had this notion I'd make you my wife."

"After having Harry killed?" Nellie cried. "You're insane if you truly believe any self-respecting woman would marry a brute who murders the man she loves most in this world."

"I figured you'd get over him in time," Killian said, relaxing his clenched fingers and looking at Fargo. "I reckon I was right. But how was I to know you're no better than a common tramp and would sleep with the first bastard who came along?"

Fargo hoped Nellie would have the sense to keep her mouth shut. He should have known better.

"Yes!" she shouted, rising. "I slept with Fargo and I'm glad I did. He knows how to treat a woman, how to be courteous and considerate. He's more man than you can ever hope to be."

That did it. Killian took a step and slapped her again, only this time she sprawled unconscious on the grass with a great welt on her right cheek. He lifted his leg to kick her, then placed it down and shook his head. "No. I have a better idea for this bitch. A much better way to teach her what happens to anyone who crosses me." He pivoted toward Fargo. "As for you, mister, you should have rode out when you had the chance."

Fargo might have jumped Killian then and there if not for the fact Curry and several other outlaws had dismounted and their revolvers were trained on him. "Speaking of chances, why don't you give me a gun and we'll settle this between the two of us?"

Killian snorted. "I'm no fool." He swung around. "Curry, tie his wrists and get him on his horse. The same with the whore, but put her on one of our horses, and have two of the men ride double back to the trading post. If either of them tries to get away, fill them with lead."

There was nothing Skye could do. He watched as three of them held the Ovaro so they could throw on his saddle, then he was bound and prodded with a rifle as he walked to the pinto and climbed up. They bundled the rest of his clothes, his guns and knife, and his other belongings into the bedroll, and one of the gang lashed the whole affair to the back of a sorrel. Nellie was revived with water from a canteen, jerked roughly to a horse, tied, and hoisted up.

"Move out!" Killian bellowed and took the lead.

The gang closed in around Fargo and Nellie, hemming them in on all sides. He wished they had at least allowed him to put his boots on. It had been ages since last he rode barefoot, and the sensitive soles of his feet would smart after a while from applying constant but light pressure on the stirrups.

Ben Killian was in a hurry. He didn't bother to stop at noon, nor did he take an afternoon break to rest the horses. Until evening he pushed hard, and when at last he called a halt at a spring he didn't appear too happy about having to make camp.

Fargo and Nellie were left to themselves while the gang members collected wood, started a fire, and tended to the stock. Two of the men went off with rifles, and a short time later a pair of shots sounded.

"I'm sorry," Nellie whispered as the outlaws bustled about all around them.

"You have nothing to apologize for," Fargo told her.

"It's my fault you're in this fix. You should have left me."

He smiled at her. "And miss all the fun we had last night? Not in a million years."

Nellie glanced at Ben Killian, who was conversing with Curry not far away. "What will he do to us?"

"I don't know," Fargo answered and leaned closer to her. "I'll do what I can to protect you, which might not be much. But you mustn't make things worse by getting him mad all the time. If he loses his temper completely, you're as good as dead no matter how much he once cared for you."

"I can't help myself when I'm near him. I want to smash his face in."

"So do I. But we have to be patient," Fargo said and tensed when a heavy footstep told him they were no longer alone.

"What the hell are you two talking about?" Killian demanded, his hands on his hips. "You're to keep your mouths shut unless I say otherwise. Savvy?"

"What will you do?" Nellie rejoined. "Shoot me?"

Fargo wanted to throttle her himself. She had totally ignored his advice. There was only so much he could do under the current circumstances, and unless she was very careful she wouldn't reach the trading post alive.

"No, bitch. I have something special in store for you," Killian responded. "Since you act like a whore I figure it's only right that you become one."

"Never!" Nellie said haughtily.

"Think so, eh?" Killian baited her and laughed. "You'll

change your high and mighty tune after I take you to San Francisco."

Curry, who was behind Killian, snickered.

"Why in the world would you take me there?" Nellie asked.

"Ever hear of the Barbary Coast, woman?" Killian asked. "It's not as wild and woolly as it used to be, but it's still a place no decent woman would be caught dead in. There are more whores there than in all the rest of California combined, and in a few weeks you'll be one of them, selling your body to any man who has the money."

"I'd kill myself first," Nellie said defiantly.

"You won't get the chance. And after we pay a visit to Chinatown and I have one of those heathen devils fill you with their opium, you won't care who touches your body. You'll lie there and let any man have his way with you and enjoy every minute of it."

Nellie's face had paled.

"I've got it all figured out," Killian boasted. "I'll sell you for a bundle and be the first one who pokes you once the opium takes effect. Just to make up for all the trouble you've given me. You should last about five or six months at your new trade, and then the opium and the men will take their toll. You'll be tossed into a pauper's grave and left to rot." He roared at the prospect.

Fargo had to admit the scheme was perfect. He knew all about the Barbary Coast, a district around Pacific and Kearny streets, a den of iniquity where life was cheap and the worst impulses in human nature were gratified for the right price. And he knew what opium could do to a person. It was an extremely powerful drug. A person under its influence often became lethargic, only half conscious, and in such a state was completely helpless.

Nellie wasn't quite cowed yet. "You'd leave your precious trading post to take me all the way there?" she said.

"I have to send a couple of wagons loaded with goods to San Francisco anyway," Killian replied. "It's been awhile since I've been there. I'm long overdue for a visit."

"So you sell the stuff you steal from the settlers there?" Fargo remarked. "Must bring you a lot of money."

106

"It does," Killian said. "And in another year I'll be rich enough to give up this life and go live in grand style in a mansion down by the waterfront."

"You'll be caught long before then."

"By who? There's no law in these parts. And the army is too far off and too busy with Indians to bother about reports of a few missing wagons. I'm not stupid, Fargo. I pick only wagons loaded with the best household goods and tools or whatever. The people in those wagons never live to tell their tales. I've only made one exception," Killian said with a telling look at Nellie. "And you can bet your boots I'll never do it again."

Their discussion was interrupted by the return of the two hunters bearing a doe. Killian walked off to issue instructions and Curry trailed him.

"What can I do?" Nellie whispered.

"Wait and hope for a chance to escape," Fargo advised. "It's a long trip to San Francisco, six hundred miles more or less. You may get lucky."

Nellie slumped, despondent. She sat hunched over, her eyes closed, immersed in her misery.

Fargo wanted to cheer her up, but words were useless. They both fully appreciated the danger they were in. He looped his arms around his legs and rested his chin between his bent knees. If Killian kept pushing, at the rate they had ridden earlier, they would reach the trading post tomorrow well before dark. Once there what would Killian do to him? He wasn't about to ask and give the butcher the satisfaction of thinking he was worried. Which he was. Ben Killian was as deadly as they came.

Soon all the horses were taken care of and a haunch of deer meat roasted over a roaring fire. The outlaws were in fine spirits, especially after Killian permitted them to take a few swigs from a whiskey bottle. They all ignored the prisoners after being told that the first man who spoke to them would be gutted with a bowie knife.

Fargo saw no sign of the Bannock, who must have gone back to his tribe after doing his job. With the advent of night the temperature lowered considerably and the cold breeze brought goose bumps out on his skin. He gazed longingly at the bundle containing his clothes.

One of the band announced that the meat was ready and the outlaws, all except for the guard who was keeping watch on Fargo and Nellie, gathered around the fire, jostling one another to be the first to get a piece. The man doing the carving couldn't slice fast enough to suit them, and they started to rip off chunks of the haunch with their hands. Killian put a stop to that and had them form into a line.

"What about us?" Fargo yelled, thinking more of Nellie than he was himself.

Killian kicked at the grass underfoot with his right boot and responded, "Pretend you're both horses. There's plenty for the two of you."

Most of the gang burst into laughter.

Fargo deliberately turned away from the fire so he wouldn't have to watch the band eat. The tantalizing odor was enough to set his stomach to rumbling and his mouth to watering. He glanced at Nellie, but she was oblivious to the world. Her spirit seemed to have been broken by the realization she was totally in Killian's power and might well end her days as a drug-addicted prostitute in a seedy section of San Francisco. And he couldn't blame her, not after all she had been through. Somehow, he must help her. But how?

For the next hour and a half the outlaws ate a lot and drank a little and related bawdy tales and jokes. From what they said, Fargo learned they were all eager to get back to the comforts of the trading post. Six men Killian picked to go with him to San Francisco the next morning were extra eager since none of them had ever been there. Curry would be in charge at the trading post until Killian came back to split the proceeds from the merchandise sold in California.

The guard was changed, the gang settled down close to the fire, and Killian brought a blanket over and draped it over Nellie's slender shoulders. "This is for her and her alone," he warned Fargo. "She won't be any use to me if she dies before we get to San Francisco. I catch you sharing it and I'll put a bullet in both of your knees." Grinning, he strolled to his bedding.

Fargo endured one of the worst nights he had ever experienced, an unseasonably cold night when the temperature dipped into the upper forties just before dawn and a wind from the northwest made it feel even colder. He huddled on the ground and shivered almost continuously. No matter how he tried, he couldn't make himself comfortable. Once he caught Nellie looking at him. She made a motion as if to hand over the blanket, but he shook his head and lied. "I'm fine. Don't worry." She curled up and dozed off.

Come morning the birds were the first to herald the dawn, as they invariably did, by filling the forest with an avian chorus. The glorious sight of the rising sun brought Fargo to his knees. He faced due east, eager for warmth, paying no attention to the gang members as they roused themselves and rekindled their fire. So it was he had no idea someone had approached until a jarring pain lanced his lower back and he was knocked forward onto his elbows and hands. Twisting, he looked up to find Ben Killian towering over him.

"I woke up in a bad mood," the gang leader said. "Reckon I'll take it out on you."

Another kick sent Fargo tumbling. The agony in his ribs nearly caused him to black out. He struggled to his knees once more, and a third kick caught him on the side of the head. Down he went, dazed and weak, hearing Nellie's shout and Killian's grating laugh, and then the kicks rained without letup and the world spun and blinked out.

11

Pain.

Pain engulfed his body and his mind, pain filled every pore, racked every nerve, more pain than most men could endure, more pain than any man *should* endure. More pain than Skye Fargo had ever known and hoped to heaven he would never know again. He knew he had revived but made no attempt to open his eyes and invite a renewal of Killian's sadistic treatment.

Gratefully, there was one bright spot in the sea of torment. He was warm, delightfully warm from his head to his toes, and the warmth compensated somewhat for the terrible pain. Luxuriating in the warmth, he lay still, listening for the conversations of the outlaws. But all was silent. He heard a fly buzz. Dozens of yards away a horse nickered, the noise muted, as if by an intervening wall.

His curiosity getting the better of him, he opened his eyes and was astonished to learn he was inside a building, apparently one of the small cabins at Killian's Trading Post, and both his wrists and his ankles were now tied securely with heavy rope. A table in the middle of the room and a chair in the corner were the only furniture. A window with a glass pane admitted streaming rays of golden sunlight that bathed his body.

He tried to sit up, but the pounding in his head intensified so badly he had to lie back down. Since he was at the post he must have been unconscious for eight hours or longer. Where was Nellie? What had Killian done with her? He gazed out the window but could see only tree branches and a patch of sky.

In the distance a guitar played and a man sang off-key.

Judging by the direction, Fargo guessed he was in one

of the cabins to the right of the trading post, probably the cabin nearest the post and directly across from Killian's house. He tucked his knees up to his chest, rolled onto his side, and pushed to his feet. Dizziness swamped him, and he stumbled and would have fallen flat on his face if he hadn't bumped into the table and braced his arms for support. His face drifted to the floor and the large stain of dried blood where his head must have been. He had lost a great deal. It was small wonder he felt extremely weak and disoriented.

Afraid he might pass out, he shoved off the table and hopped awkwardly to the chair. Sitting, he had to close his eyes to ward off more vertigo. His mouth was exceptionally dry; he couldn't even form enough moisture to lick his lips. And whoever had tied him had done so thorough a job that his circulation in his arms and legs had been cut off. Because of his movements they began tingling, increasing the discomfort.

In the trading post a woman laughed gaily.

Did anyone other than Killian's crowd know he was there? he wondered and doubted it. Killian wouldn't want the word to get around, especially as the butcher intended to kill him sooner or later. He was quite surprised to still be alive and wondered why Killian hadn't finished him off yet.

He had to get out of there and find Nellie. Raising his arms, he studied the rope binding his wrists. Without a knife it would take some doing but his teeth should suffice. He applied his front teeth to the knots and patiently worked away, slowly undoing first one knot and then another until the rope was loose enough to be cast off with a shrug of his arms. He was about to do so when boot steps crunched on the dirt beyond the door and someone fumbled at the latch with a key. Instantly he slid to the floor and scrambled a yard from the chair, then lay quietly with his eyelids cracked, holding his arms so the rope wouldn't slip off his wrists.

Into the cabin came Curry and two other men. "Roll him over," Curry instructed, and the pair stepped forward to flip Fargo none too gently onto his back. He feigned unconsciousness. He might learn important information if they thought he hadn't revived.

"The boss figured he'd be up and around by now," commented the taller of the henchmen.

"Maybe he has been," Curry said, looking suspiciously at the chair. He raised his right knee to waist level and held his boot over Fargo's head. "If he's faking we'll know in a second. I'm going to turn his ear into a pancake."

Fargo opened his eyes. Nothing would be gained by pretending any longer, and he was rather fond of his ear. "Where is your boss?" he asked. "I'd like to tell him what I think of anyone who beats on a helpless man."

Curry slowly lowered his leg and hooked his thumbs in his gunbelt. "I knew it," he gloated. "I figured you had come around. Hardly anyone ever uses this cabin, but the dust on the chair was all smeared."

"Pretty sharp," Fargo said. "Maybe you should be the brains of this outfit."

"I can still stomp your head in if you keep sassing off," Curry threatened. "And you can forget about talking to Killian. He left for San Francisco this morning."

The news shocked Fargo. It meant he had been unconscious about twenty-four hours and explained why he felt so unusually weak. Hunger and the great loss of blood had rendered him a shadow of his former self.

"As for your sweetheart," Curry said, leering, "she squawked like a mad hen when they dragged her into the wagon this morning and tied her hands and feet. She was sore because Killian wouldn't take her up on a bargain she wanted to strike."

"A bargain?" Fargo said when Curry stopped and waited to be prompted.

"Yeah. She wanted Killian to let you go in exchange for her promise to let him do what he pleased with her. She even claimed she would marry him if you were set free." Curry chuckled. "The bitch didn't take it too kindly when the boss pointed out that he could do as he damn well pleased with or without her say-so."

The other outlaws chortled.

Curry nudged Fargo with a boot toe. "As for you, Killian gave me orders on what to do. Come nightfall we're going to take you into the gorge." He paused. "Do you remember that Bannock who found you and the Lee woman?"

Fargo nodded.

"His Injun name is Flint Tongue, or something like it, and he's a hellion. Likes to carve his enemies up bit by bit and listen to them scream for mercy. He acts as Killian's go-between with the Bannock tribe, setting up meetings and such," Curry said. "You'll be tickled to know Flint Tongue is starting the festivities tonight by cutting off all your skin while you're alive to appreciate it. I hear he plans to make it into a pouch for his woman."

"Any chance we can call it off until tomorrow night?" Fargo asked. "I'm not feeling too well." He let his shoulders slump to give the impression he was much worse off than he actually felt at the moment, which was terrible.

Curry grinned. "I like a man who can go on making jokes when he only has a few hours to live." He straightened. "Wiley, you and Sam watch our guest while I fetch more rope. We don't want him up and moving about before the party tonight." Wheeling, he ambled out.

Fargo was lying between the two men. He yawned as if greatly fatigued and casually lifted his hands to run them through his hair, being careful not to let the rope slip off yet. Both gunmen were ignoring him. He would have one chance and one chance only and if he failed he would certainly die at the hands of the bloodthirsty Bannock. So he had everything to gain and nothing to lose by suddenly sitting up, throwing the rope off his wrists as he did, and driving a fist into the groin of each hired killer. Knowing exactly where to hit to do the most damage, he doubled both men over, bringing their heads within easy reach. He grabbed each by the back of the hair, then slammed their faces together. Not once, but twice. The outlaw called Wiley tried to pull loose but couldn't. As their grimy faces crunched together the second time, both men sagged to their knees, enabling Fargo to snatch their revolvers. He smacked each across the bridge of the nose with a barrel and the two men toppled backward, Wiley groaning loudly.

Fargo put down the revolvers and tore at the rope around his ankles, his fingers shaking with exhaustion. If Curry came back before he could get the rope off he was a goner. His ears strained for footsteps as he worked frantically. There were three knots. The top one resisted him the longest, and once it was untied the others quickly followed. He put a hand under him and rose, then stooped to pick up the revolvers. His dizziness returned with a vengeance, causing him to sway unsteadily.

Outside someone was yelling.

He dearly wanted to strip a shirt and boots off one of the men, but he dared not take the time. Shuffling to the doorway he peeked out and saw a pair of Killian's whores standing near the trading post. No one else was around. Unfortunately, the only horses were tied to the hitching rail in front of the post and trying to steal one of them would get him gunned down since the post was where most of Killian's men would be. Taking a breath, he walked boldly out and turned left, stepping to the corner on his aching feet. When the corner was behind him he breathed again and made for the forest.

Curry's voice rang out from near the house, telling someone to hurry up with a rope, as Fargo entered the trees and hastened up a gradual slope. Every step brought agony. He avoided thickets and fallen limbs although once he stepped on a sharp twig that cut into his sole and started the foot to bleeding. Stretching away from the rim of the slope was a wide plain dotted with pines, birch trees, and some cottonwoods. He had no choice but to hike across it. To go north would bring him too near the gorge. To go south would put him too close to the approach to the trading post from the Oregon Trail.

A gully offered concealment and he slid down into it, tearing his other foot on a jagged rock. Limping now, he hurried eastward as best he could, tapping his innermost reservoir of strength just to stay upright. He heard a lot of shouting and knew Curry had discovered he was gone. It wouldn't take more than a couple of minutes to get every man at the post out searching for him. If the Bannock was there he'd be tracked down in short order. If not, the outlaws would have to rely on sight.

He had a thought. How many of Killian's gang were left? Originally there had been about fifteen or sixteen. He'd killed five, if he recalled correctly. Killian had said something about taking six men with the wagons to San Francisco. That left only four, not counting Curry, and perhaps a few more if the total had been higher. He felt a spark of renewed confidence. The odds weren't as lopsided with Killian and those others gone.

Where the gully ended he climbed out and sank onto his stomach in high grass behind a cottonwood. His body craved rest and the cool grass was so inviting he rested his forehead for a few seconds. Weariness washed over him like a tidal wave, and his mind went blank. With a start he realized he was falling asleep and jerked his head up again. If he dozed off they would find him, sealing his fate. Through sheer force of will he got his limbs in motion, stood, and staggered eastward.

Skye concentrated on his legs to the exclusion of all else. As long as they held out he might escape. He laboriously lifted first his left, then his right, and forged onward, wincing sometimes as he stepped on a sharp stone or a dead branch. From the position of the sun he knew it was close to noon.

He lost track of the distance he covered. When his feet and legs were throbbing and he couldn't go another step, he sought shelter in a stand of birch and sank gratefully down with his back against a tree trunk, facing toward the trading post. He saw no one yet and was surprised. Maybe the outlaws were hunting near the buildings in the belief he was too hurt to travel very far.

Although he would rather have sat there forever, he rested only a few minutes before goading his reluctant body into going on. He hadn't tramped but a few yards when he tripped and smacked his left shoulder into one of the birch trees. But what was one more pain when he ached all over? Grinning inanely, he plodded across a clearing and into a stand of pines.

Finally, yelling erupted on the plain. He stopped, knelt behind a small pine that had branches low to the ground, and peered out. Approximately two hundred yards off were Curry and the gunmen making a wide sweep. They wouldn't come anywhere near his hiding place for another five minutes or more.

He was surprised at how much ground he had covered. Dropping onto all fours he worked his way through the pines until an open field appeared. Flattening, he crawled to the left, intending to swing around the field into heavy brush beyond, when he heard his name being shouted by Curry.

"Fargo! Give up and we'll go easy on you! I'll personally put a bullet in your head instead of turning you over to Flint Tongue. What do you say?"

The man was all heart, Fargo wryly reflected and kept crawling. Curry must be getting desperate, with good reason. If he escaped there would be hell to pay when Killian came back from California. The idea pleased him. He hugged the trees, then crawled through grass a couple of feet high, being careful not to rustle the tops of the stems more than the breeze was already doing. He was halfway to his goal when a new sound reached his ears, and he immediately stopped.

Someone was running through the pines.

Twisting, Fargo extended both revolvers and cocked both hammers. He saw a gunman appear and scan the field, and it took a few moments for recognition to dawn. The gunman was his old friend Shanks who still sported a number of black-and-blue bruises from the savage beating administered by Killian the other night. He aimed his right-hand pistol, or tried to, but he couldn't hold the barrel steady. Annoyed, he gritted his teeth and tried once again.

Shanks seemed to guess that their quarry was close at hand. He took several steps into the field, then halted and scoured the landscape in all directions.

Fargo didn't so much as blink, which in his severely weakened state was difficult to do, except to move the revolver as Shanks moved, keeping the barrel fixed on the outlaw's chest. A bead of sweat trickled down his brow and into his left eye, making the eye sting as if it had been poked with a thorn, partially blurring his vision. It was then that Shanks turned toward him and advanced three strides, peering intently into the grass.

He didn't know if Shanks had spotted his vague outline or not, and he didn't dare wait to be certain. Once the gunman saw him, Shanks would dive for cover and be harder to hit. So he gripped the revolver firmly, touched his finger to the trigger, applied slow but steady pressure, and felt a tingle of satisfaction when the gun boomed and Shanks catapulted over as if kicked by a Missouri mule.

Now the rest would converge on his position. He lurched upward and ran, his legs balking, his feet exquisitely painful. There were yells to his rear and somewhere a gun cracked. The bullet missed but not by much, thudding into the ground a yard away and sending a fine spray of dirt flying. He plunged into a thicket, the branches tearing at his clothes and face, and barreled through until he rushed into the open. Slugs crisscrossed the thicket, one buzzing past his head like an angry hornet.

He ran as best he could, every stride torture. There were no more trees for hundreds of yards. The ground was flat and lacked adequate cover. Once Curry and the other killers reached this side of the thicket they could easily pick him off. Already he was becoming winded. A ball of intense pain formed in the pit of his stomach and worsened the farther he went. His breath came in ragged gasps. When he spied a hollow not more than two feet deep and five feet long he dashed over to it and lay flat on his back.

The shouting was much nearer.

"He must be up ahead there!" one of the killers was saying.

"Watch your ass. He killed Shanks," said another.

Curry chimed in with, "I don't give a damn about taking the son of a bitch alive anymore. Fill him with holes."

"With pleasure," someone declared.

Fargo pegged their positions by the sound of their voices and knew they must be within twenty yards of where he lay. They wouldn't be able to see him until they were right on top of the hollow so he might be able to get one or two before they discovered him. After that—he was at the mercy of fate. Running was out of the question. In his shape he couldn't go ten feet without collapsing.

He cocked the right revolver again and rolled onto his side. Cautiously raising his head, he spotted Wiley to the south. To the north was the gunman named Sam. None of the others, including Curry, was visible. He sighted on Wiley, the closest, and waited. Both men were gazing farther east, thinking he must be up ahead.

Fargo's chin sagged, his eyelids drooped. He could barely focus. Determined not to cave in, he propped his elbow on the ground to hold the gun level. Wiley filled the sights and kept on coming, and when Skye was one hundred percent sure he fired. The slug ripped into Wiley's gut, bending the killer over as he involuntarily screamed and pumped three rapid shots in Fargo's direction. None scored. Again Fargo squeezed off a shot and this time Wiley pitched onto his face.

Sam had sought cover and was firing at the hollow. Elsewhere, Curry and two more opened up. Dirt rained down on Fargo as their bullets struck too close for comfort. He snapped off another shot, but his fingers were sluggish, his aim awful. Then he heard Curry bellow an order that brought a chill to his battered, anguished body.

"He can't get us all at once! Rush him! Now!"

And on they came.

12

Skye Fargo saw four killers charging toward him and knew he had reached the end of his rope. He fired at the one named Sam. The gunman, hit, drew up short, then rushed forward. Fargo rose to one knee. If he was going down he would go down fighting to the last. The revolvers felt unbearably heavy and it was all he could do to point them.

Above the blasting of the revolvers there suddenly thundered the retort of a large caliber rifle. One of the outlaws was sent sailing a good three feet to smash onto his face in the grass. The others, except for Sam, stopped in confusion and looked every which way, trying to find the source of this new, unexpected threat.

Fargo fired both revolvers simultaneously at the on-rushing Sam. This time his shots were more effective. Sam jerked when struck, then keeled over.

Curry motioned with his arm, the signal for his men to press the attack, but he took only a single step when the rifle thundered and another of the outlaws died. Whirling, Curry fled with the sole remaining gunman, the pair weaving until they reached the pines at which point they sprinted flat out into the trees and vanished.

Puzzled, Fargo turned to the north, to where he figured the rifle shots had come from, and saw a buckskin-clad form rise and walk toward him. It was the grizzled mountain man from Fort Hall. "You!" he exclaimed, smiling. "What the hell are you doing here?"

Peterson paused. "That's a fine how-do-you-do for the man who saved your hide from those mangy coyotes." He grinned and advanced, cradling an old Hawken rifle in his arms. "Now we're square for you lending a hand at Burke's."

"I'm glad you came along when you did," Fargo admitted, staring westward to see if Curry might be inclined to try again. He glimpsed the two gunmen briefly, running strong, before the vegetation swallowed them up. "Another minute and I'd be worm food."

"A minute, nothing," Peterson said. "Ten seconds would be more like it. They had you dead to rights." Stopping, he studied the big man from top to bottom. "What in tarnation happened to you? You look like you fell off a cliff and landed on a grizzly."

"Ben Killian," Fargo said.

"Oh," Peterson responded grimly. "Should have guessed. When you rub him out, give him a lick for me."

"I will."

The mountain man stepped up and put a friendly hand on Fargo's broad shoulder. "You look like you're about to fall over. Why don't you stay here while I fetch my horse and my mule. Won't take but a couple of minutes."

"I can manage," Fargo said. "Lead the way."

"You sure are a tough cuss," Peterson said and began retracing his steps. "We'll go off in the hills until you heal up. I'll lend you—"

"No," Fargo interrupted. "I can't go anywhere. All I need is some food and water, a few hours of sleep, and I'll be as good as new. Then I'm going back to the trading post."

"Killian will have you stretched out for the buzzards."

"He's not there. He left this morning for San Francisco and took a woman he'd kidnapped with him," Fargo revealed.

"So that explains it. I happened to stop by Fort Hall and heard from that Texas boy, Harkey, about his partner. He told me you were fixing to put Killian out of business so I decided to ride on over and see if I could be of help. Stopped by the post last night for a drink but didn't see you nor Killian either."

"How long did you stay?"

"At the post? Most of the night. There were a few pilgrims from a small wagon train there, and I sat in on a game of cards. Won a couple of dollars," Peterson said. "Why?"

"You might have saved my life last night too," Fargo said. "Killian was all set to turn me over to a Bannock called Flint Tongue. He probably held off with you nosing around and told Curry to have me taken care of tonight."

"Flint Tongue? I know that murdering dog. Always wanted to add his scalp to my collection."

They hiked for several hundred yards. Toward the end Fargo moved at a turtle's pace, drops of blood dripping from his left foot.

"I've got me an old beaver skin I can cut up and wrap around those feet of yours," Peterson proposed. "Otherwise you'll be hobbling on crutches before too long."

The horse and mule were in a wash, the mule burdened with enough supplies for two animals.

"This is Lilly," Peterson introduced her. "For God's sake don't stand behind her or she'll kick you plumb to the moon. She's the most contrary critter that ever lived, and I've got the scars to prove it."

Fargo sat down on a flat rock and placed the revolvers at his side. "If she's so mean why don't you get rid of her?"

"She reminds me of me," the mountain man replied with a grin. "Besides, she's the only one who listens to me when I take to rambling. That fool horse doesn't even pay attention."

Men who lived alone in remote corners of the mountains often became quite fond of their animals, as Fargo knew, so he didn't laugh at the idea of someone earnestly talking to a mule. One old prospector, so the story went, even took to dressing his burro in a dress he made himself, calling her "sweetheart," and letting her sleep in his cabin at night. Everyone swore he was crazy. But was it coincidence that the warlike Utes, in whose country the man had found a vein of ore, left him to his burro and his diggings in peace?

Peterson brought over a full canteen. "Don't be shy," he said. "I've got another and there's a spring a little ways to the northeast."

"Thanks," Fargo said, and drank half the contents in greedy gulps. The water, tepid though it was, revitalized him almost instantly. He lowered the canteen and wiped the back of his hand across his damp mouth.

"I don't have much grub," Peterson said. "Usually hunt my meals when I'm hungry, but I like to keep some jerked meat handy in case I can't." He brought over a beaded parfleche, a type of pouch used by various Indian tribes. "Help yourself."

Inside was a pound of dried and salted bear meat. Fargo pulled out a strip and ate with relish. He no sooner finished one piece than he grabbed another.

"I reckon I'll have to shoot me another bear first chance I get," Peterson remarked.

Fargo's teeth couldn't chew fast enough. He was ravenous, as if he hadn't eaten for a week instead of a day. He stuffed his stomach until it hurt and he couldn't take another bite. Lowering the parfleche, he drank more water, polishing off the canteen.

"You ever eat a buffalo at one sitting?" Peterson asked.

"No, but I ate a whole cow once," Fargo said, leaning back on his hands and squinting at the sun. As much as he wanted to settle accounts with Curry, he needed a little rest before returning to the post. "Wake me in two hours."

"I ain't got no watch but I'll do the best I can. And don't fret none. I'll make sure Curry doesn't ambush us while you're sawing logs."

Confident the mountain man would be as good as his word, Fargo reclined on his back, draped a forearm over his eyes to blot out the sunlight, and fell promptly asleep.

A rocking motion gave Fargo the illusion he was astride a horse until he realized he was rocking from side to side, not rising up and down. He heard a name being insistently repeated, his own name at that, and struggled to collect his swirling thoughts. Suddenly he remembered everything. He opened his eyes and sat bolt upright.

"Took you long enough," Peterson said, taking his hand off Fargo's shoulder. "I've been trying to wake you up for ten minutes or better. Shook you so much I about wore out my arm."

Fargo looked at the sun. It was the middle of the afternoon, giving him plenty of time to do what must be done. He saw the parfleche lying where he had placed it and removed a handful of bear meat.

"You're eating again?" Peterson asked in disbelief.

"Maybe I should go hunting and see if I can rustle us up an elk or two."

Grinning, Fargo took a bite. "This will tide me over for now." He gazed in the direction of Killian's. "Any sign of Curry while I slept?"

"Nope. If he only has a few men left, he'll play it smart and wait for you to come to him. You'll be walking into a trap."

"I know."

"Then I hope you don't mind some company. I promised Lilly I'd buy her a whiskey."

"Your mule drinks?"

"Doesn't every mule?"

While Fargo ate more meat and drank water from Peterson's other canteen, the mountain man used his bowie to cut an old beaver hide into two sections, wrapped them around Fargo's lacerated feet, and tied the hides fast with leather strips.

"There," Peterson said, standing. "That ought to hold you for a spell."

Fargo stood to test how well he could walk. The hide, soft and supple, fit his feet as nicely as a pair of moccasins and he moved about with ease. "This is fine," he said and gave the parfleche back to his newfound friend.

"Are you fixing to settle accounts?"

"I am," Fargo answered, retrieving the revolvers. He checked both cylinders and found a single unspent round in one gun and three good rounds in the other. "I don't suppose you have any ammunition I could use?"

"Sure don't. Sorry," Peterson said. "I don't pack a pistol myself. For long range I have my Hawken, and for close-in fighting I rely on my bowie. Neither have failed me yet."

Fargo wedged the revolvers under his belt. "I'll just have to make every shot count." He regarded the old man for a moment. "You don't have to help. This is my fight and I can handle it."

"Like I said, I promised Lilly a drink," Peterson responded and nodded at his horse. "You're welcome to ride if you wish."

"I'll walk," Fargo said, wanting to unlimber his muscles to be ready for the upcoming gunfight. He hiked westward and Peterson, leading the horse by its reins and the mule by its lead rope, fell into step beside him.

Words were unnecessary. Both men were fully alert and braced for trouble. Near the basin they slowed, Fargo with both revolvers out, Peterson with his Hawken cocked. At the rim they squatted and glimpsed the trading post, the cabins, and the large house through the trees.

"Looks awful quiet down there," the mountain man commented.

Fargo nodded and glanced toward the gorge, which couldn't be seen from where they were, wondering if Killian had posted a new lookout to replace the man he'd slain. If so, the lookout should have noticed him escaping earlier and given a yell to Curry. Possibly, that high up, the lookout had assumed he was one of the gang. He glided silently down the slope, the makeshift beaver shoes muffling his tread.

Peterson, leaving his animals ground-hitched, followed.

There was no movement in the vicinity of the buildings. Fargo darted from trunk to trunk until he came to the last tree. The trading post appeared deserted. There was no laughter, no music. And the horses at the hitching rail were all gone. Not for a second did he believe Curry had fled. The gunman had only run off earlier because of Peterson's timely intervention. Curry was crafty enough to have known he bucked a stacked deck by trying to tackle a concealed marksman. Now it would be different. Curry had the advantage.

Fargo broke from cover and raced to the rear of the cabin where he had been held. He was nearly there when a shot cracked high on the gorge and the slug hit the ground a few inches from his right foot, proving there was a lookout to be dealt with. Reaching the wall, he stopped to catch his breath. The roof screened him from the lookout so he was momentarily safe.

But Peterson had disappeared.

He scoured the trees but saw no trace of the mountain man. Puzzled, he edged to the corner and dared a peek at the trading post. Instantly the man on top of the gorge fired, and the bullet smacked into the wood less than an inch from his face. He pulled back, then worked his way around the cabin to the southwest corner. Across from him reared Killian's house. Left of that was another cabin. There was no movement at any of the windows, nothing to indicate there might be a gunman lurking within.

Somehow he had to reach the trading post. The house was a half-dozen yards closer to the post than the cabin sheltering him, so without hesitation he broke into a run, making for the south side. He covered barely six feet before the lookout opened up and a puff of dust in front of his toes let him know how close the shot had come. Breaking into a zigzag pattern, he succeeded in getting two-thirds of the way to the house.

The rifleman on the gorge tried again. No sooner did he fire than another rifle answered, a louder rifle in the trees to the east.

Fargo attained the south side as a scream fell on his ears. He glanced at the gorge and saw a man tumbling end over end from the high rim. The lookout struck a boulder at the base, bounced once, and lay outstretched with his legs bent at an unnatural angle. Fargo ran along the house, ducking under the windows he passed, until he reached the rear corner.

A back door hung partly open.

He jogged to the doorway and stopped clear of the jamb, listening. So far as he knew only Curry and one gunman remained. Were they both waiting in the post or was one or the other in the house? He had to find out or risk being shot in the back as he approached the post.

Fargo kicked the bottom of the door with his right leg and the door swung inward, revealing a small kitchen no doubt furnished with more items stolen from slain settlers. Beyond the kitchen lay a hall. He darted in and to the left, then crouched with the revolvers leveled. Nothing stirred. The house resembled a tomb.

He warily crept down the short hallway and discovered stairs leading to the upper floor and a spacious living room. About to turn and go upstairs, he spotted an open closet and went over to check. There were shirts and pants hanging from pegs, and in one corner, piled in a heap as if they had been tossed in there and then forgotten, were his shirt, hat, and boots. He removed them, and as he lifted the shirt he found his gunbelt, his Colt, and the Arkansas toothpick lying on the floor. Evidently Ben Killian had decided to keep the weapons and effects for himself.

Fargo quickly donned his clothes, removed the beaver hides, and slipped his feet into his boots. It was a tight fit, as both feet were slightly swollen and rather painful, but he felt better having them on. Next he strapped on the knife and the gunbelt. Standing, he poked his head in the closet again on the off chance there might be more guns. In a near corner, hidden by a coat, was his Sharps. Unfortunately, it was unloaded and there were no cartridges. He leaned the rifle against the wall near the front door, making a mental note to come back and get it later.

Checking the Colt, he found it loaded, then he twirled the revolver and smiled. The familiar feel of the pistol was reassuring. He left the other two revolvers lying on the floor. While they were fine guns, he was accustomed to his and a man always preferred a weapon he used regularly and had practiced with for countless hours over a strange gun or knife.

Now he moved swiftly, confidently, to the foot of the stairs and paused. From above came a faint rustling noise, like the rustling of a woman's dress as she walked. He cocked the big .44 and took the stairs two at a stride. In front of him appeared a hall with a door on either side, both closed. He flung open the door on the right first and discovered a bedroom, the huge bed unmade, the blanket rumpled and hanging off the near side. He saw no one. Striding to the left-hand door, he shoved it wide. An open window explained the rustling noise: a breeze from the west was moving the curtain.

Fargo turned toward the stairs. Out of the corner of his eyes he detected movement in the first bedroom, and he instantly crouched and spun on his heels. A pistol blasted. A bullet smashed into the wall above him. He spotted an arm protruding from under the bed, from under the overhanging blanket, and squeezed off three shots, aiming at the space between the bottom of the bed and the floor.

The arm went slack and the revolver fell from limp fingers.

Slowly, cautiously, Fargo entered the bedroom and

prodded the blanket with the toe of his boot. There was no reaction so he dropped onto his left knee and lifted the blanket with his free hand. Under the bed, three holes in his cheek, was the gunman who had fled with Curry.

Now only one remained. The top gunman himself.

Fargo stood and walked to the top of the stairs, ejecting the spent cartridges as he went, certain Curry was waiting in the trading post and would have the front approach covered. On the top steps he paused, about to insert a new cartridge into the cylinder, when two distinct clicks at the bottom of the stairs made him freeze and glance down.

Smirking up at him was Burke, and in the portly man's hands was one of the most feared weapons west of the Mississippi, a double-barreled shotgun.

13

Skye Fargo had looked down the lethal barrels of shot-guns before. He knew that at close range they were virtual cannons. One twitch of Burke's fingers would blow him in half, so he didn't so much as twitch a muscle as Burke laughed and placed a foot on the bottom step.

"Look at this! The great Skye Fargo caught with his pants down," Burke said and hefted the shotgun. "I've dreamed of a moment like this ever since you humiliated me, you bastard. Now the shoe is on the other foot. How does it feel?"

Fargo made no comment.

"I think I'll start at the knees and work my way up. The buckshot in this thing will take you apart chunk by chunk," Burke said and cocked his head. "No. On second thought I'll put my first shot right there," he stated, training the twin barrels on Fargo's groin.

There was one slim chance. If Fargo could throw himself backward before Burke fired, most of the buckshot might miss. He tensed his legs for the attempt.

"I'll earn my money this month," Burke went on, apparently enjoying the situation. "Bet you didn't know that Killian pays me a tidy sum to direct business his way?"

"I knew," Fargo said.

Burke straightened in surprise. "What? How did you know?"

"It wasn't hard to figure out. Why else would the owner of a trading post send his customers to another one?"

"You mean those dumb cowboys? Sure, I talked them into it, them and a hundred more just like them. Cow-boys and settlers are all the same to me, just stupid sheep waiting to be fleeced. And no one can shear them better than Ben Killian," Burke gloated.

Inching his left heel back, Fargo was all set to jump when a shadow fell on Burke from the rear. Either it was Peterson, in which case his fat would be pulled out of the fire, or it was Curry, in which case the fix he was in just became worse. But when a voice addressed Burke he knew both of his guesses were wrong.

"Turn, you polecat. I ain't never shot a man in the back yet, and I don't aim to start with worthless trash like you."

Burke blanched, gripped the shotgun tighter, and whirled, spinning to the left and whipping the shotgun around. He was way too slow. A revolver boomed and Burke tottered as a hole sprouted between his eyes. The shotgun tilted at the floor and discharged with a devastating blast, ripping a jagged hole in the floorboards. Burke began to fall as the revolver fired a second time, the slug tearing into his neck. He was dead before he crashed onto his back, his vacant eyes fixed on the ceiling.

"That's for my pard, you son of a bitch."

Fargo rushed down the stairs. Between the hall and the open front door stood Harkey, swaying slightly, a smoking gun in his right hand. Fargo glanced at Burke and said softly, "Never rile a Texan. You're just asking for trouble."

"Howdy there, Fargo," Harkey greeted him, the words noticeably slurred. "Where's the rest of this bunch? I'm here to make them pay for what they did to Lester."

Reloading as he walked, Fargo went up to the young cowboy. "I thought you were going to sober up?"

"Hell, I'm not drunk. I just took a nip to steady my nerves. I'm a cowpoke, not a man-killer." His gaze drifted to the corpse. "At least I wasn't until a minute ago." He swallowed. "Now where's the rest of this outfit?"

"Killian headed for California this morning with six of his men. The only one left is Curry, and you're in no shape to go up against him."

"Curry is here?" Harkey said, and began to turn. "Good. He's the one I want the most. He killed poor Les."

"No," Fargo said, grabbing the Texan's arm. "Leave him to me. You've done enough."

"Not by a long shot," Harkey said, trying to pull free. "So let go and point me in Curry's direction."

Fargo released his hold and shrugged. "All right. If you want to get yourself killed I won't stop you. But I think Lester will roll over in his grave when he sees you acting like a jackass."

"What do you mean?"

"Do you think Lester would want you to throw your life away? That's what you'll be doing if you go up against Curry. You know it and I know it."

"But I've got to do something. Les was my best friend, the best pard any man ever had. We grew up together. Always worked together. He was closer to me than my own brother. I have to do something," Harkey said.

"You already did," Fargo replied, pointing at Burke. "And you did me a favor by showing up when you did. Now let me pay you back by taking care of Curry."

"I don't need anyone to fight my fights for me."

"This is my fight too," Fargo said. "Curry was fixing to have a Bannock torture me. I have as much right to him as you do. So let me tangle with him first. If he wins, he's all yours."

Harkey pondered for a bit. "All right. But I'm only doing this because you've asked me. I ain't scared of him."

"Never claimed you were," Fargo said. He walked to the front door and saw Peterson beside the cabin in which he had been held. The mountain man gave a little wave and indicated the trading post. Fargo nodded and motioned for Peterson to stay where he was. Then, the Colt in his right hand, he advanced toward the post.

As he neared the entrance he heard the sound of playing cards being ruffled. At the doorway he paused to scan the bar and the tables. The only person present was Curry, seated at a table on the left and playing solitaire. He entered and halted. "You're card-playing days are over."

"I've been expecting you," the gunman said, unruffled. "Figured it would be you and me eventually."

"Stand up."

Curry made no move to comply. He deposited a red

queen on a black king, the deck held loosely in his left hand, his right hand free. "What's your hurry to die?"

"You have it backward," Fargo said. "And I'm going after Killian as soon as I'm done here."

Putting a black four on a red five, Curry nodded. "He had a feeling about you, a bad feeling. That's why he sent for Flint Tongue the day after you paid us your first visit. He was going to have the Injun track you down and kill you before you could cause us any trouble, but then you went and took the woman." He looked up. "Never saw him so mad in the two years I've known him. He wanted her for himself."

"So I was told," Fargo said, suspicious of the way the gunman was stalling. He glanced at the doors at the back of the establishment but they were closed.

"Never could see what made her so special, myself," Curry commented. "We were taking a big chance by letting her live. If it had been up to me she would have been killed when her husband was." He sighed, let the cards fall onto the table, and slowly stood, his gaze on Skye's Colt. "You aim to shoot me down like a rabid dog or do it fair?"

"Fair," Fargo answered, sliding the Colt into his holster. "Unlike you, I don't kill men who can't defend themselves."

"You mean the woman's husband? I had Shanks put his own gun on the table for the sodbuster to use. The idiot went and made a grab for it, too."

"Then whenever you're ready, make a grab for yours."

"It's your life."

Fargo waited, willing his body to relax, his hand poised near the .44. If he tensed up his reaction time would actually be slowed and he'd be more prone to make a mistake. By holding himself loose but ready his reflexes would automatically take over the instant he saw Curry's hand twitch.

"Once word of this gets around I'll be more famous than Jack Slade," Curry said.

Slade, Fargo knew, was a gunman acquiring quite a name for himself down near Julesberg. He also knew Curry was trying to distract him to gain an edge. But he refused to fall for the ruse.

"So I should thank you for being so obliging," Curry

went on. "It isn't every day that—" he continued and suddenly went for his gun while still speaking, in the middle of his sentence when it would least be expected. His right hand swooped to his ivory-handled revolver, and he executed a lightning draw.

Fargo was faster. The Colt belched lead and smoke, the slug ripping into Curry's chest, the impact hurling him backward into his chair. Both crashed to the floor. Fargo stepped quickly forward. Curry was on his hands and knees, struggling to rise. The gunman looked up, then began to raise his gun. Fargo's second shot caught him in the forehead and he collapsed.

"Nice shooting."

Fargo turned, lowering the revolver. Peterson was framed in the doorway, the Hawken pressed to his shoulder. "I wanted you to stay out of it."

The mountain man grinned. "Always did have a mind of my own. Ask anybody. They'll tell you I'm the most contrary cuss who ever wore britches."

There was the sound of running, and Harkey appeared at Peterson's shoulder. He stared at Curry's body and nodded in satisfaction. "You did it. Good. Now Lester can rest easy in his grave."

Fargo walked to the bar, removing the pair of spent cartridges as he did, then paused to reload and holster the Colt. Stepping up to the shelves of liquor he said, "Name your poison."

Peterson and Harkey came over.

"Give me a whiskey," the mountain man requested.

"The same here," Harkey said.

Fargo poured for all three of them. He was raising his glass to his mouth when furtive footsteps and muffled voices sounded outside. Resting the glass on the counter, he shifted toward the entrance and touched his hand to the Colt just as a woman's face materialized. She peeked inside, spied Curry, and her mouth fell open in astonishment. Then she disappeared and there was the murmur of excited conversation.

"We have company," Peterson said dryly.

Harkey drew his gun. "Should we run them off, old-timer?"

"Are you loco?" Peterson rejoined. "We have this whole place to ourselves and I'm in the mood for some fun. Why, we could have ourselves a regular party. Think of it."

The Texan did, a sly smile curling his lips as the full implications hit home. "Dog my cats! You're right. I reckon I can hold off going to Oregon for a few days."

Fargo took hold of his glass again. He saw the same woman boldly step into the doorway and regard the three of them critically, her hands on her hips. "Join the party," he said, holding the glass aloft. "There's plenty for everyone."

"We're not coming in until we know what you plan to do with us," the woman responded. She nodded at Curry. "None of us want to wind up like him."

"You're in no danger," Fargo assured her. "Our fight is with Killian and his men, not you."

"When Ben gets back there will be hell to pay. He'll turn over every rock to find you, mister, and when he does your life won't be worth beans."

"Killian won't be coming back."

The woman studied him a moment, then frowned. "Great. Just great. And what the hell are we supposed to do? We're stranded here unless our money is still in Killian's safe."

Harkey had politely doffed his hat. He rather shyly moved toward her and gestured at the bar. "Why don't you ladies come on in and have a drink with us, and we can talk over how to help you gals out? I'd be honored if you'd let me help you get to wherever you're of a mind to go."

"Count me in," Peterson said.

"We'll take you up on your kind offer," the woman said and glanced to her right. "It's safe, girls. Come on in." She sashayed to the bar trailed by the five other doves.

Fargo began pouring more drinks. "Where have you ladies been?" he asked.

"Curry shooed us all out earlier," answered a slim young blonde. "He said there was going to be trouble and he didn't want any of us to catch a bullet." She bobbed her head to the north. "Took us into a gorge out yonder and ordered us to wait until he came for us."

"We got tired of waiting," said another. "It was hot

and there were bugs all over." She frowned. "I hate bugs."

"I liked those horses we saw," offered yet a third dove. "Especially that fine black-and-white stallion. I think it was one of them Appaloosa horses that those Nez Perce Indians use all the time."

"It's an Ovaro," Fargo corrected her, relieved to learn Killian hadn't taken the pinto, and gazed at the door to Killian's office. The mention of the safe had sparked his curiosity. He left his drink on the bar and walked the length of the trading post. Since he had learned long ago never to take anything for granted, he drew the Colt before opening the door. The office was empty and in the southeast corner sat a squat safe. He walked over and yanked on the large handle but couldn't budge it.

"You'll need a hammer and a heavy chisel to get it open."

Fargo glanced around to see Peterson leaning on the jamb. "Any idea where I could find them?"

"I dabble in prospecting from time to time," Peterson disclosed. "Have a hammer and a couple of chisels packed on Lilly. Want me to fetch 'em for you?"

Fargo nodded and when the mountain man hurried away he rose and rummaged through Killian's desk. There were a few coins in a bottom drawer along with an almost full bottle of rye. Another drawer contained an old dragoon and a hunting knife. In the top drawer were five sheets of paper containing long lists of various items: guns, tools, tack, clothes, and even food. Some of the items had been crossed off, others had not. He realized the sheets must be Killian's inventory of stolen merchandise and wondered if the goods crossed off had been sold or otherwise disposed of. The sheer quantity amazed him. Having dealt with wagon trains before, he knew that many settlers packed their wagons to overflowing with burdensome possessions they refused to leave behind and enough supplies not only for the long trip but to tide them over in their new home as well. Some wagons contained thousands of dollars worth of goods. It was easy to see how Killian had amassed so much in such a relatively short span of time.

He was going over the lists carefully in search of items that might have been taken from the Morelands' wagon but had found nothing specific when Peterson hustled back into the office.

"These should do," he announced, holding up a metal mallet and a pair of sturdy chisels.

They set to work, taking turns. Peterson went first, applying the tapered end of the chisel to the top hinge on the door and pounding with the mallet for over twenty minutes before he tired and offered them to Fargo. Forty minutes later, as Fargo was taking his second turn, the chisel bit through the last strip of hinge and the door abruptly sagged, the bottom corner digging into the floor. He gripped the handle and tugged, managing to lift the door half an inch and pull it outward the width of his hand. It refused to budge any further so he attacked the bottom hinge with renewed vigor.

Peterson took over eventually and worked but a few minutes when the hinge gave way and the door fell with a tremendous clang. He had to leap aside to avoid having his toes crushed.

Fargo squatted to inspect the contents—two thin shelves piled high with documents and papers. He sorted through the upper shelf while the mountain man did likewise on the bottom shelf. Many of the papers were personal letters written by scores of different people and not one was addressed to Ben Killian. There were certificates of birth, several wills, a few diplomas, and an envelope crammed with both preferred and common stocks frequently traded on the New York Stock Exchange.

"What do you make of all this?" Peterson asked.

"These papers belonged to the settlers Killian has killed," Fargo deduced, frowning because he had found nothing belonging to the Moreland family. "Don't ask me why he'd keep them."

"I was sort of hoping we'd find some money."

Fargo placed the envelope on the top shelf, his brow knit in deep thought. If, as Rosie and the saloon girl maintained, Killian always kept a lot of money in the safe, then Killian must have cleaned out all the currency before leaving for California. But why? Did Killian always take his ill-gotten gains with him because he didn't trust his hired killers to leave the safe alone? Or was there a better reason? Could it be that Killian had no intention of coming back to the Snake River region? Had

Killian decided his murderous enterprise had become too risky and cleared out for good?

"What are you thinking about?" Peterson inquired.

"I'm thinking it's time I found my horse and lit out after Ben Killian."

"Care for some company?"

"No. You stay and help Harkey get the women out of here. And you might want to ride to Fort Hall and check on Rosie and Flo," Fargo said. He stood and hitched at his gunbelt. "Leave Ben Killian to me."

14

Eighteen hours later Skye Fargo was crossing an arid plain, riding to one side of the clearly marked ruts left by the four heavy wagons Killian was taking to San Francisco. From the depth of the ruts he knew the wagons were loaded to capacity with stolen possessions Killian would sell in California, and he was glad the greedy bastard had taken so much. The wagons would make slow progress, enabling him to overtake them well before they reached the California border.

He had been in the saddle since before sunup and felt tired and sore. Twice he had stopped briefly to rest the Ovaro. Now the stallion was in need of another rest, and he scoured the plain for any hint of water or grass. Twisting, he even gazed at the country he had just covered on the off chance he had missed a water hole. Instead of water he spied a dust cloud perhaps a mile off. Someone was following him.

Fargo drew rein. The size of the cloud told him there was more than one rider, probably four or better, and they were pushing to catch him. Since Peterson and Harkey would be tied up with the women for days, it wasn't them. Nor could it be any of Killian's crowd because, so far as he knew, they were all dead with the exception of the six men with Killian. Who did that leave?

He lightly jabbed his spurs into the Ovaro's flanks and galloped beside the wagon ruts. Hills in the distance promised a place to take cover if he could only reach them. The pinto, though tired, didn't flag. He settled into the rhythm of its movements and rode until the hills reared directly ahead. Sweat beaded his forehead and caked the stallion when he reined up and checked on his pursuers.

They were less than three-quarters of a mile off now.

The wagon track bore to the south, but Skye took to the barren hills. There were few trees, little brush, and occasional patches of grass, none of which offered concealment. A trace of a game trail, perhaps made by deer or bighorn sheep, wound up and over the hill he was on and he took it to the crest. Halting, he shielded the sun from his eyes with his hand to better see the men on his trail. There were four and they were Indians.

Bannocks.

He went down the slope and between another pair of hills, then stopped when he spotted a rock ledge forty feet up on the hill to his left. The going was steep, but he got the Ovaro to the ledge and slid down. Taking the Sharps, he stepped to the edge and sank to one knee, then loaded a cartridge. The angle was ideal. He was in a perfect position to pick off the warriors as soon as they appeared, and they would be hard pressed to hit him.

Fargo sighted on the gap and cocked the rifle. He heard the drumming of hoofs, but a second later they ceased. Mystified, he lifted his head to listen, but all was quiet. He heard the sigh of the breeze, nothing else. A full minute passed yet the Bannocks did not appear. Two minutes went by. Three. Had they given up the chase? He doubted it. Did they know, then, that he was waiting for them? It seemed impossible at first thought, but then he saw the drifting tendrils of dust the Ovaro had raised when climbing to the ledge, tendrils that were floating in the gap between the hills. If he could see them, so could the Bannocks. And if they had, then they would avoid the gap and come over the hill.

He stood and whirled, the Sharps held at waist height. A brave was perched on the rim above, an arrow notched to a bow, the string already pulled back. Instantly he tilted the barrel upward and fired, not really expecting to score, as the brave let the shaft fly. He dived to the right, landed on his side, and rolled to his knees. The Indian was gone, apparently unhurt, while the arrow had struck the ledge, glanced harmlessly off, and sailed a dozen yards to embed itself in the dirt below.

Fargo held the rifle in his left hand and drew the Colt. He backed toward the Ovaro, anxious to get off the ledge. So long as he stayed there he was a sitting duck.

The bucks could pick him off at their leisure. A painted face poked into sight, and he snapped off a shot to discourage another try on his life. Then he jammed the Sharps into its scabbard, grasped the saddle horn with his left hand, and pulled himself into the saddle while training the revolver on the rim.

Yanking on the reins, Fargo spurred the stallion from the ledge and down to the bottom of the hill, raising a cloud in his wake. An angry whoop let him know the Bannocks had seen. He glanced back to discover two of them on horseback, coming over the top of the hill. Where was the other pair? A glance at the gap showed them racing to cut him off. One of them he recognized; it was Flint Tongue.

Rather than go straight he angled to the left, hunched low to make it harder for them to hit him. Flint Tongue's revolver cracked twice. Something plucked at his hat. Then he was going all out, the Bannocks whooping in fury. He came to another hill and went around it. Before him unfolded another expanse of plain offering nowhere he could make a stand.

Fargo knew the fleet Indian ponies might overtake the tired Ovaro before long. He also knew the Bannocks were expecting him to continue to flee. They would sweep around that last hill, their blood lust aroused, eager for the chase. So he did the exact opposite, the last thing they would expect yet the one thing that might save his life. He hauled on the reins and brought the stallion to a sliding stop, then turned and charged.

Flint Tongue appeared first, shrieking like a banshee. He saw the big man bearing down on him and blinked in surprise. Reining up, he tried to bring his revolver into play.

A blast from Fargo's Colt sent the renegade toppling. A second buck swept past Flint Tongue, using his legs to guide his mount as he lifted a bow to take aim. Fargo put a slug in the man's chest. The last two Bannocks weren't inclined to carry on the fight. They abruptly wheeled and sped off, one of them clinging to the side of his horse so he wouldn't be shot.

Skye let them go. Giving chase would needlessly further tire the Ovaro and waste time better spent catching up with Ben Killian. And by the time they reached their village and reported the clash he would be long gone. So, with a parting glance at the prone Flint Tongue, he wheeled the pinto and rode south.

Once out of the hills he struck the wagon wheel ruts. Killian had skirted the hills, then swung to the southwest, the general direction of San Francisco. He did the same, holding the stallion to a mile-eating canter. The condition of the ruts, the loose dirt that had been blown into the tracks and the smooth upper edges, made it clear he wouldn't overtake his quarry before noon or later tomorrow, causing him to chafe with impatience. Images of what Killian might be doing to Nellie formed a perpetual frown on his face. He couldn't wait to get the son of a bitch in his gun sights.

A rare glade at the base of a mountain was his camp site for the night. He allowed the stallion to drink at a small spring, then slaked his own thirst and prepared a pot of coffee. Before leaving the trading post he'd taken the liberty of stocking up on the supplies he needed and now had enough coffee to last him half a year. His saddlebags also contained a pack of jerked beef, but he didn't have much of an appetite.

The night seemed unending. He tossed frequently and woke up at the faintest of sounds. Several times he rose and surveyed the country ahead, hoping in vain to spot the glow of a campfire. Well before dawn he was up and saddling the pinto. After a hasty cup of coffee he resumed the hunt.

Five hours of riding brought him to a stream. This was where Killian had camped. Using a rock he poked around in the remains of their campfire and found warm embers at the bottom. A short rest and he was on the go once more, certain he was only an hour or two behind the wagons.

The sun climbed past its zenith. A mountain range appeared, the trail leading straight for it. He wondered how Killian intended to get the ponderous wagons to the other side and figured Flint Tongue had revealed the location of a pass or another way to get through. The ruts took him to the mouth of a green valley, and he drew rein on spying a column of smoke beyond a tract of woodland.

Fargo pulled the Sharps out and loaded it. Then he

cautiously entered the valley, slanting to the left where the undergrowth was thickest. In the shadows the stallion's black-and-white coat blended perfectly into the background, so if he went slowly there was slim chance of being seen or heard by the outlaws.

The acrid scent of their fire indicated when he was close, and shortly the sound of gruff laughter reached his ears. Dismounting, he tied the reins to a tree limb and padded forward on cat's feet until he spotted figures moving about. Then he dropped into a crouch and worked his way close enough to overhear a conversation taking place.

". . . don't care how hard it is. I want the wheel fixed in an hour. If it's not, I'll hold you accountable, Morton," Ben Killian was saying.

"We'll do the best we can," replied a lanky man wearing two guns who was the only person Fargo could see clearly. "But it's going to take more than an hour. We have to find the right wood, then trim it—"

"I don't want to hear your damn excuses!" Killian cut him off. "Just do it."

Skye flattened and snaked to where he could observe the wagons and all the gang members. The Conestogas were strung out in a row, their teams at rest, saddled horses tied behind every wagon but the second one. Disabled by several broken spokes and a splintered rim on a front wheel, the third wagon sat tilted at a sharp angle. Three of the outlaws were examining the break. Two others were unloading tools from the first wagon. Morton, scowling in anger, was walking toward the crippled Conestoga. And not twenty feet from Skye stood the top man himself, Ben Killian. Where was Nellie? Skye mused, worried by her absence.

He wasn't surprised one of the wagons had broken down. As burdened as the Conestogas were with more weight than they were designed to carry, it was remarkable there hadn't been a problem previously. A competent wagon-boss would have brought along a few spare wheels just in case, but Killian had trusted to luck and lost.

To Fargo's relief Nellie Lee suddenly appeared at the back of the second wagon. She glared at the outlaws, then bestowed a look of sheer contempt on Killian.

"Do you suppose I can stretch my legs awhile? I've been cooped up in here so long I'm starting to sprout feathers."

Killian laughed and beckoned for her to come out. "I reckon it won't hurt. But don't get any fancy notions in that pretty head of yours. If you try running off you won't get fifty yards, I can guarantee you."

Nellie clambered to the ground and smoothed her dress.

"Yes, indeed," Killian said, blatantly admiring her assets. "You'll bring a fine price even if you are used merchandise."

"Go to hell!"

"Is that any way for a proper lady to talk?" Killian retorted, smirking, and jabbed a finger at her. "You're a hypocrite, woman. You pretended to be the grieving widow and put on airs of being prim and modest, but then you went and spread your legs for the first yack who came along."

Her temper flared, her features becoming crimson. "Skye Fargo is more man than you can ever hope to be!" she responded. "He stirs a woman deep inside like you never could, you disgusting brute."

Ben Killian took several strides toward her, then checked himself, his fists clenched. "Be careful, bitch. I don't let anyone insult me. Keep it up and you'll be sorry."

"I'm scared," Nellie said sarcastically.

"You would be if you had any brains," Killian snapped and walked to the third wagon.

Fargo watched Nellie move slowly toward the trees in which he was hiding, her head held low, her shoulders slumped in dejected defeat. Killian glanced at her and said something to one of his men who then turned and watched her intently. If she tried to flee they would be after her in a flash. He cocked the Sharps, being careful to muffle the noise by holding his cupped left hand over the hammer, and sighted on Killian. If the top dog was downed the rest of the pack might scatter, making the rescue easier.

Taking methodical steps, Nellie had drawn within fifteen feet of the woods. Her back was to the wagon and there were tears in her eyes. Although she was putting on a good front, her despair was transparent.

Fargo held the sights steady on Ben Killian, who had knelt to look at the damaged wheel. Normally he wouldn't even think of shooting a man from concealment, but these were exceptional circumstances. He didn't dare confront the outlaws while Nellie was still in their clutches; or she might be slain in the cross fire. Or, worse yet, Killian might kill her out of sheer spite. First he must spirit her to temporary safety, then deal with Killian's bunch.

Nellie was now ten feet off. She stopped, dabbed at her eyes, and shifted to stare at the wagons.

Fargo raised his head just enough to whisper, "Nellie! Don't let on you know I'm here!" He saw her back stiffen but otherwise she didn't betray his presence. "Move toward me and act natural," he directed. "And whatever you do, don't look into the trees."

She clasped her hands and turned, tilting her head to stare at the sky. As if entranced by the clouds she strolled closer and began to whistle.

Fargo frowned. She was overdoing it and the man watching her was sure to notice. A second later the outlaw took a step and lifted an arm.

"Hey! That's far enough!"

Fleeting panic lined Nellie's face and she bolted, darting toward the woods.

"Hey!" the outlaw repeated.

Fargo decided to act. His finger curled around the trigger and he squeezed off his shot, but at the precise instant he fired at Killian the man watching Nellie took another pace, stepping squarely into his sights. The slug tore into the outlaw's midsection and he was thrown backward to sprawl on top of Ben Killian and another member of the band.

Shoving erect, Fargo drew the Colt as Nellie ran to his side. Killian was trying to untangle himself with the help of two other men. A third killer had his revolver out and was already taking aim. Fargo fired from the hip, two rapid shots, and the killer jerked as if dancing on the end of a puppeteer's strings, then collapsed.

"Oh, Skye!" Nellie cried, seizing his left arm.

"Run!" Fargo said, tugging free and giving her a shove

that caused her to stumble and almost fall. "I'll be right behind you," he added and took off on her heels. A pair of outlaws were racing from the wagons, and he discouraged them with two more shots, one of which ripped through the swiftest man's neck, stopping him cold. The brush plucked at his clothes and branches stung his face, but he ignored both and instructed Nellie to bear a little to the right.

No pursuit had yet materialized when they halted beside the stallion. Fargo quickly shoved the Sharps into the scabbard and swung up, then lent a hand to Nellie. Rather than ride out of the valley, which Killian would most likely anticipate, he made for the jagged peaks rimming the valley to the south. There was shouting at the wagons, Killian bellowing for his men to mount and go after Nellie. He broke from the woods, crossed a narrow meadow, and sought sanctuary in a tangle of thickets.

"Oh, Skye," Nellie whispered, clinging to him as if to life itself, her body rubbing against his with the friction of their motion. "I thought I was done for."

"We're not in the clear yet," Fargo advised.

"How did you get away from Curry? Killian has been gloating ever since we left his trading post that by now you had been carved into pieces and fed to wild animals."

"I'll tell you all about it later," Fargo said, listening for the beat of horse hoofs. His diligence was rewarded by the crashing of underbrush back in the trees.

"Where the hell are they?" someone yelled.

"This way!" answered another.

"No, this way!" said a third.

Fargo stopped, partially turning the pinto so he could spy anyone after them. More crashing arose in the trees, growing fainter as the riders headed toward the mouth of the valley, assuring him they had eluded the killers for the time being. He continued toward the peaks, aware of Nellie's cheek resting on his shoulder and her breath on his neck.

A sheer cliff eventually barred his path and he turned to the right, moving among huge boulders. There were clefts in the rock, some deep, others shallow. A quarter of a mile farther on he found one that nearly qualified as a cave. The opening was just wide enough to admit a horse, and inside it broadened out to the size of a typical parlor.

Fargo reined up. The cleft was an ideal place to hide out. Unless someone was riding past it, the inner area was invisible. And enough sunshine filtered in the entrance to provide adequate light. "We'll stay here awhile," he announced and lowered Nellie to the ground. Climbing down, he took the reins and began to lead the Ovaro through the narrow opening. The stallion balked, disliking the confined space, but obeyed after he stroked its neck and spoke softly. He let go of the reins and the pinto moved off to one side.

"Think they'll find us here?" Nellie asked as she came through the opening.

"I doubt it," Fargo answered. "By the time they realize they went in the wrong direction and circle back, it will be too dark for them to track us even if they could."

"What do you mean?"

"I doubt any of them can track an elephant across a muddy field," Fargo said. "Tracking is an art. It has to be learned like everything else. And few hired killers take the time to learn it." He saw Nellie nod. Then, without warning, she hurled herself at him and wrapped her arms around his shoulders in a passionate embrace as she planted her lips on his and kissed him with an intensity that defied belief. He responded slowly, surprised by her desire, and when she finally broke the kiss he regarded her with amusement. "What was that for?"

"For saving me from that fiend," Nellie replied huskily. "It's my way of saying thanks. And there's more where that came from."

"Now is hardly the time—" Fargo started to object when she molded her body to his and kissed him again, her warm hands on his cheeks, her ample breasts grinding into his chest. He gently rested his hands on her shoulders, about to push her off, to inform her he still had to deal with Ben Killian, when it occurred to him that Killian stood an even chance of winning. This might well be the last time he would ever know the thrill of making love, the last time he would relish the sensations a naked female form aroused in him. Rather than push her away, he returned her embrace with equal fervor, his hands exploring the small of her back and her buttocks. She trembled when his fingers slipped into her crack.

Nellie seemed to have cast off all her inhibitions. Her tongue fenced with his, her bottom thrust hard against his loins, while her hands roved up and down his body.

Fargo felt fingers close on his manhood and his shaft, at half-mast, sprang to its full length. He cupped her breasts and squeezed, massaging her nipples with his palms, feeling their heat through her dress. She ran a finger along his organ and his throat constricted. With an almost savage gesture he yanked her dress high and slipped his left hand between her smooth legs. She was hot, so hot and ready, that she quivered and cooed in his ear.

He sought her slit and inserted his forefinger. Her hips bucked, her lips swooped to his neck. Inserting a second finger into her throbbing portal caused her to arch her spine and gasp. He hastily unfastened the buttons at the top of her dress and greedily descended on her globes when they burst free. Her taut nipples were like sweet candy.

"Oooohhhh," Nellie breathed. "You make me . . . ," she said and groaned when his fingers plunged deep into the well of her being, leaving the thought unfinished.

Feeling as if his organ would tear through his leggings at any moment, Fargo fumbled at his belt until his engorged pole leaped out, his pulsing tip flush with her pubic mound. Her hand curled around him and a moan escaped his lips. Then she did the unexpected. Nellie eased down until she was on her knees and her moist mouth curled around his manhood. The sensation was exquisitely delicious, more potent than the strongest drug, a natural high eclipsing every other known to man. His head fell back and he closed his eyes, marveling at her instinctive skill, at the manner in which she would bring him to the peak of ecstasy and hold him there for a bit before tempering her lust to allow him to regain some semblance of self-control.

Nellie groaned as she slurped, her hands straying around his iron thighs to grasp his bottom, her nails slicing into his sensitive skin. It was as if she was trying to devour him, as if his organ was a loaf of bread and she was famished.

He checked his need as long as he could. Ultimately, he jerked her upright, their mouths clung together, and he hiked her dress again to gain access to her heavenly center. Both of them were slick with wetness and hot with unrestrained desire. His organ found her opening and in an automatic rocking motion he thrust himself to the hilt inside of her. They froze, locked in carnal union.

"Oh God!" Nellie suddenly cried. "It's now! It's now!"

Skye had a tornado on his hands. She thrashed and heaved and ground into him, her arms over his shoulders, her lips parted as she panted mightily. Her upheaval took him unawares, giving him no chance to gird his loins and ride out the storm so he could spend when he was ready. His manhood pulsed to the beating rhythm of his racing heart and twitched uncontrollably, a prelude to the deluge to come. He kissed her, grabbed her breasts, and squirted like a fire hose gone berserk.

"Uuuuuhhhh! Yes, honey! Fill me!" Nellie wailed.

Fargo did, several times over. And all the while they coupled in a sublime frenzy, in the back of his mind a tiny voice warned him that he should be thinking about his upcoming confrontation with Ben Killian, a confrontation from which only one of them would emerge alive.

15

Three of the wagons were gone.

Skye Fargo rode out of the trees with his Colt in hand. A quarter moon afforded enough illumination for him to see only the disabled wagon remained. Killian and his three henchmen must have headed for California and left it behind. Why? That was the question he pondered as he dropped to the ground to examine the tracks. There had to be thousands of dollars worth of stolen items in the disabled wagon, and he couldn't see Killian simply abandoning it.

And why had Killian gone off without making a more determined effort to find Nellie? After all the boasting Killian had done about how much money he would get when he sold her, it didn't make sense for him to ride away and just leave her.

Fargo found the ruts and ran his fingers over the impressions. His best guess was that the wagons had departed within the past couple of hours. He should be able to catch them before morning. Sliding the Colt into its holster, he climbed on the pinto and headed out. He thought of Nellie, back at the cleft, and felt certain she would be safe until he returned. He had given her the Sharps and plenty of ammunition, plus his canteen, coffee, and jerky. She could subsist on the grub for days if need be. The only wild animals capable of harming her were bears and cougars, and from the lack of sign there were few of either species in the immediate area. Nor were the Bannocks likely to find her. If she stayed put she would be all right.

Even so, he toyed with the idea of going back for her. If he was to be killed, she would be stranded in the valley. Her only way out would be to hike to the Oregon

Trail and hope a wagon train came by. She might make it, she might not.

He had to make damn certain he returned to take her to safety himself. And the sooner he settled accounts with Killian, the sooner he could come back. If she was along now the added weight would slow the pinto down and he would have the added burden of worrying about her the whole time, a distraction that could prove costly once the fight began.

The wagons had gone down the valley and out the other end. He halted to check the tracks every so often in case Killian had turned aside, but their course stayed constant. Where the valley gave way to a mountain range he stopped once more and crouched to feel the earth for ruts. They were there, bearing to the southwest. He started to rise when a rifle thundered and his hat flew from his head. Releasing the reins, he took a running leap and came down on his stomach with the Colt in his right hand.

An unnerving stillness had gripped the night.

Fargo took stock. He was in a clearing, partially screened by tall grass. Ahead reared a towering mountain. On both sides were walls of forest. Since he hadn't glimpsed the muzzle flash he had no idea where the rifleman was hiding. All he could do was wait.

He was more worried about the stallion than his own hide. The Ovaro had started back into the valley when he let go of the reins and had halted after going less than thirty feet. It was standing in the open, waiting for him, and he feared the rifleman might decide to kill the horse to leave him stranded afoot. Thankfully, the minutes ticked by and the pinto went unharmed.

Why had there been just one shot? he asked himself. If Killian and all three gunmen were out there somewhere, they would have fired a volley to increase the odds of slaying him on the spot. Instead, a single rifleman had tried to kill him, leading him to conclude Killian had left only one man to do the job.

When ten uneventful minutes passed, Fargo took the initiative. He crawled to the north until he was under the trees, then rose in the shelter of a wide trunk. Either he stayed where he was until daylight, allowing Killian to put more distance between them, or the hunted became the hunter and he went after the rifleman. A mental image of Nellie, alone and anxious, made up his mind for him.

He glided from tree to tree, the mountain his destination. If he had been given the chore he would have selected a high spot to give him an advantage, so it was a safe bet the gunman was on the slope above. At the edge of the forest he paused to study the lay of the land. Boulders and trees offered abundant places for the killer to lay low. Flushing him without being spotted first would be extremely difficult.

Not that he had a choice. The killer was bound to be watching the Ovaro, waiting for him to try and mount up and escape. Perhaps that was the reason the stallion still stood. Bending forward, he dashed up to a boulder and scanned the terrain above. The feeble moonlight failed to penetrate the deeper shadows, of which there were scores, and in any one the rifleman might be silently poised to fire. He moved to another boulder and knelt, wincing when his right knee bumped a rock. Again he scoured the darkness; again there was nothing.

About to rise, an idea struck him. It was literally one of the oldest tricks in the book and only a greenhorn would fall for it. Or a gunman whose nerves were stretched to their limits by the strain of waiting alone in the night to kill a man with a reputation for being as stealthy as an Indian and as deadly as a coiled rattler. He picked up the rock in his left hand, hefted it to better judge the weight, then heaved with all of his strength. The rock crashed into a pine tree twenty yards away.

Sixty feet up a rifle flashed.

Fargo held his fire. The range was too great for an accurate pistol shot in the dark. He must get closer. Turning to the right, he carefully climbed until he was about level with the rifleman. Now he began to stalk in earnest, easing onto his elbows and knees, then lying flat and working his way toward where he hoped the killer was hiding. If the man had moved, he was in trouble.

It took a minute to go a foot. Every move had to be slow and precise and he dared not make a noise. The outlaw would cut loose at the crack of a twig. He broke out in a sweat despite the breeze and felt his palm become clammy. He went ten feet. Then fifteen. Beside a bush he paused, breathing lightly.

Something rustled among boulders ahead.

Had the gunman shifted position or had it merely been an animal? Fargo groped the grass with his left hand until he located another fist-sized rock. The trick might not work again, but if it did he saved a lot of time. He swept his arm back and threw the rock to land below the boulders concealing the rifleman. There was a loud thud, a clattering noise, and a muffled curse from the boulders. He had the killer pinpointed. Unfortunately, this time the man wisely held his fire. Now the killer knew Fargo was nearby and would be scanning the slope all around.

Fargo put the lessons he had learned from the Sioux and other tribes to good use. His body might as well have been a log. Eyes locked on the boulders, he waited and hoped the gunman would make a mistake.

The wind picked up, stirring the pines.

He was reminded of how the Sioux had taught him to lie by a game trail for hours on end without scratching or shifting, although blinking once every five or ten minutes was allowed. To an Indian the time was of no consequence. And since most warriors had a wife and children depending on their hunting ability, they acquired skills deemed impossible by the majority of white men. Moving silently, sitting or lying for four or more hours under a burning sun, going days without food and water—these were all endured by braves with as much indifference as the white man paid to the weather.

A vague figure popped up among the boulders.

Fargo already had his right arm extended. He aimed quickly but wasn't quick enough. The gunman dropped from sight again. On the off chance the man would reappear at the same spot, he held the barrel steady. Nothing happened. He resigned himself to a long stay on the mountain and relaxed his finger on the trigger. Then he heard another sound, one he couldn't identify right away. With a start he realized small stones were rattling down the slope on the other side of the boulders, which meant the rifleman was on the move, perhaps heading for his horse to get out of there.

Damn it! Fargo fumed and sprinted toward the boulders, knowing if he was wrong he could expect to feel burning lead tear through his body. Skirting to the left, he saw the gunman in full flight thirty feet down, almost to some trees. He raised his arm, sighted, and fired.

The trees engulfed the rifleman.

He dropped at the base of a huge boulder as the rifle banged, his arms over his head for protection from the stone slivers that rained down when the slugs ricocheted off a few feet overhead. A chip stung his cheek. Another nicked his neck. He could hear the gunman crashing through the brush and rose into a crouch. The man had too much of a head start, but he had to try. He ran down the slope to the trees, then stopped.

A horse was galloping hell bent for leather to the southwest.

Fargo sighed and jogged toward the Ovaro. At least he should be grateful the stallion hadn't been shot. Once in the saddle he rode in the direction the wagons had been going. Although the run-in with the rifleman had delayed him, he was still confident he would soon overtake Killian. Not even a lunatic would try taking loaded wagons through a mountain range at night, and Ben Killian wasn't crazy no matter what Nellie might believe. A cold-hearted killer and as calculating as they came, yes, but undeniably sane.

There had to be a telltale fire somewhere, Fargo kept telling himself. The wagons couldn't have gone more than ten miles, if that far. So sooner or later he should spot the glow from their campfire. But after riding six miles or better and seeing no trace of it, he slanted up a slope on his right and climbed until he enjoyed a panoramic view of the surrounding countryside. The terrain was bathed in the pale moon glow. Otherwise, there were no lights anywhere. Either the fire was remarkably well concealed or Killian had made a cold camp.

Fargo decided the outlaws were playing it safe and had not bothered to make a fire. If he pressed on he might pass them without knowing it. In order to prevent that from happening, he descended to where he felt the wagon tracks should be and climbed down to feel all around the ground. He felt grass and earth and twigs and stones, but no ruts. Annoyed, he straightened and debated his next move.

He must already have gone past the wagons. Killian

had likely turned into a side canyon or a valley to await daylight. And because he had been so intent on catching the bastard, he'd failed to stop and check for the ruts every so often as he had done earlier. Now he either waited for dawn himself or continued his search. With Nellie Lee alone back at the cleft, he couldn't afford to wait.

It was tedious work, having to stop to listen or to dismount and search for wagon tracks. He retraced a mile of the route he had taken, then two miles. Fatigue nibbled at his mind, and he fought off an impulse to find a sheltered spot to rest. Going around a stark peak resembling an enormous inky needle, he halted yet again and climbed down. Squatting, he ran his left hand over the grass and discovered the familiar outline of a rut almost immediately. Excited and wide-awake, he traced a curving track that led toward woods to the south.

Rather than make of himself a better target by riding to the trees, he walked, the reins in his left hand, the Colt in his right. The trees presented a solid wall of closely spaced trunks, and he didn't see how the wagons could have penetrated very far into the woods. Upon drawing nearer he discovered an opening and a ten-foot wide ribbon of grass and weeds that separated two sections of forest, a path adequate enough for wagons to use. His probing fingers confirmed there were tracks leading in so he moved to the left, hugging the trees as he advanced.

The ribbon meandered for a considerable distance until the trees ended and a small valley nestled between towering mountains unfolded before his searching gaze. He sank to his left knee, trying to read the lay of the land. There were stands of trees scattered about the valley floor and the wagons might be behind or in any one of them. Since Killian probably had a man posted to stand guard, Fargo rose and walked to one side where high weeds and thickets offered a suitable spot to ground-hitch the pinto.

Moving to the center of the valley, he cat-footed from cover to cover, alert for alien noises. But it was a scent that made him stop short and focus on a section of ponderosa pines to his right, the bitter scent of fresh horse urine borne on the cool breeze. Imitating a snake once more, he worked closer, pausing when he heard a low whinny. Were the wagons in there, or was this another ambush arranged by Killian?

He bore toward a particularly dense cluster of pines, then halted when another scent tingled his nose. This time it was cigarette smoke. So someone was awake and would have to be dealt with first. He lifted his head and tested the breeze, trying to fix the gunman's position. When he turned his head to the left the smoke was weak. To the right it was stronger. He moved to the right.

Like a human bloodhound he closed on his prey. Suddenly a tiny red dot in the midst of the pines showed him where the gunman was concealed and he swung in a wide half-circle to come at the man from the rear. Under the trees he had to be extra careful not to put any pressure on fallen branches or to rustle the grass. In twenty minutes he was directly behind a skinny man who was leaning against a ponderosa pine, a rifle tucked in the crook of an elbow, while puffing on a cigarette.

Skye Fargo rose slowly, took three measured, silent strides, and jammed the barrel of his Colt into the back of the outlaw's neck. "If you move I'll blow your spine in half."

The gunman went rigid, the cigarette dangling from his parted lips.

"Let go of the rifle," Fargo directed, taking the gun in his free hand and tossing it aside. Next he yanked the outlaw's pistol out of its holster and threw it after the rifle. Stepping to one side, he pointed the .44 at the man's head and said, "Face me. If you try to warn your boss, you're dead."

With a nervous bob of the chin to demonstrate he understood, the outlaw pivoted and elevated his arms. "Don't shoot," he said, the cigarette in the corner of his mouth. "I ain't about to die for Ben Killian."

"What's your name?" Fargo asked.

"Richter."

"Where's Killian?"

"Up the valley a ways," Richter revealed. "He's with the wagons. Morton and me were told to wait and if you showed to kill you."

Fargo peered into the ponderosa pines. "Where's Morton?"

"In the trees about a hundred yards southeast of here," Richter said. "Killian wanted us scattered out so you couldn't get by." He cocked his head like a rooster inspecting a kernel of grain. "What happened to Wilson?"

"Who?"

"The hombre Killian had waiting for you near that big valley. I thought I heard shooting awhile back and he never showed up. Figured you had done him in."

Fargo found the news interesting. Wilson must have lit out for parts unknown rather than rejoin Killian. "We traded shots and he got away," he admitted.

Richter digested the news. "Smart man," he said, then abruptly winced and said, "Damn!" The cigarette had burned down nearly to the end and seared his upper lip.

"Get rid of the smoke," Fargo commanded and saw the gunman take it in his left hand and move his arm as if to fling it to the ground. The next instant the cigarette was flying at his face, sparks shooting at his eyes, and he ducked, realizing he had been played for a fool. Richter pounced, and Skye let himself be tackled and knocked onto his back, releasing the rifle as he fell. Since a shot would alert Morton and Killian, he clubbed Richter across the nose with the Colt and when the outlaw tried to jerk out of harm's way he struck him again.

Richter dived to the right, his right hand clawing at his shirt, trying to pull it out from under his belt.

"Freeze!" Fargo snapped, but it was no use; the gunman wouldn't listen. Richter yanked the shirt out and grabbed an object tucked under his belt, and although the shadows didn't permit Fargo to see the object clearly he intuitively knew it was a spare gun, a hide-out kept handy for emergencies. He rolled and lunged as Richter tugged the revolver out and clubbed the outlaw a third time with his Colt. Richter, on his knees, swayed but brought the gun up.

As much as Fargo wanted to end their struggle quietly, he had to shoot or die so he shot, a single retort that rippled off across the valley. The Colt spat lead and smoke, and Richter flipped backward as if slammed in the head with a club. Fargo stood and stepped to the body. A dark hole over Richter's right eye testified to his accuracy. Irritated, he gave the corpse a kick, then picked up the rifle and edged to the end of the pines.

More trees were visible off to the southeast, perhaps the very stand where Morton lurked. Both the two-gun killer and Killian now knew he was close. They would be ready for him.

It didn't matter.

Fargo stalked deeper into the valley.

16

As every Apache learned at an early age, there was an art to sneaking up stealthily on a man expecting to be attacked. Each Apache boy was taught how to use any available bit of vegetation and the contours of the ground to his advantage. He learned how to creep from bush to bush like a lizard, how to blend into the background like a snake, and how to charge with the unexpected suddenness of a cougar. Each boy was instructed in how to contort his body so that at night his outline would be mistaken for a small boulder or a bush. Apaches were, as anyone who had ever fought them would attest, undisputed masters of crafty stealth.

To a lesser degree so were the braves in other tribes. And since Fargo had spent so much time among them, including the Apaches now and then, he had learned a few tricks of their lethal trade. He used them all now as he approached the second stand of ponderosa pines. One minute he would be slithering like a bull snake along a depression, and the next he would be crouched on all fours beside a shrub, for all intents and purposes another plant himself.

All Fargo's effort was getting him nowhere. He hoped to spot Morton before the outlaw spotted him, but when he had reached a point within twenty feet of the pines he still had not located the gunman. Either Morton was an old hand at this sort of thing and knew how to camouflage himself perfectly, or else Morton was no longer in the trees.

Fargo made for a large log and once behind it stopped to rest. He would have been inclined to think Morton had left if not for the utter lack of night noises in the ponderosas. Not so much as a cricket chirped. There had to be something—or someone—in the trees that had made all the insects fall silent. He crawled to the end of the log for a look and peeked out.

Gunfire shattered the quiet, the twin blasting of twin revolvers booming in cadence.

Fargo recoiled as pain flamed across his temple and along his neck. The world spun and for a moment he thought he would pass out. He rested his forehead on his forearm as the gunfire ceased. His ears rang terribly. He touched his fingers to his temple and they became sticky with his blood.

Wicked laughter cut the night. "The great Trailsman my ass!" a gruff voice declared, followed by silence more profound than before.

Morton would be coming after him! Cursing himself for being the biggest idiot west of the Mississippi, Fargo forced his limbs to move. He rolled away from the log into grass, then scrambled in a beeline to the south, thinking he would crawl all the way around the stand.

Those twin revolvers cracked again, splitting the night with lead and flame.

Fargo recoiled as slugs thudded into the earth all around him. Somehow, Morton knew exactly where he was! If he didn't move he was bound to be hit. He shoved upright, staying bent at the waist, and ran awkwardly toward the south side of the stand, the pain in his temple impairing his coordination. A bullet nicked his left leg. Another took a chip out of his boot heel. And then the ground suddenly opened up and he pitched headlong into a gully.

For several more seconds bullets buzzed overhead. Finally the twin guns fell silent.

Fargo rolled onto his back, grunting when a pang lanced his skull. He was in serious trouble. Morton wasn't a run-of-the-mill gunman; his accuracy and senses were amazing. How the hell did the man know where he was all the time? His own night vision was better than average but this Morton must have eyes like a cat. He'd known a few men in his time, whites and Indians, who could see at night almost as well as most people could see during the day. Maybe Morton was one of them.

He couldn't stay put. Morton would be hunting him, would find him in no time. He rose, squatting while he took his bearings, and discovered he had dropped the rifle somewhere along the line. Palming the Colt, he stretched out until he could peer over the gully rim. Nothing moved in the ponderosa pines. Ducking low, he moved to the end of the gully closest to the trees, braced his feet to give him added momentum, and broke into a run.

Morton had shifted position. His guns thundered off to the right.

Fargo hurled himself to the left, working the hammer twice, hastily aiming his shots at the spot of darkness between the twin muzzle flashes. He landed on his side, fired again as Morton stopped shooting, then darted into the pines where he stopped beside a trunk. His injured temple pounded terribly, so much so he couldn't hear a thing other than the drumming of his own blood in his veins. If Morton was closing in he wouldn't know it until too late.

He knelt and licked his dry lips. Gradually the pounding subsided. His hearing returned to normal. For a minute there was the murmuring of the breeze through the branches above his head, and then an odd, strangled laugh from the vicinity of where he had last glimpsed Morton. The laugh changed to a wheezing cough followed by a drawn-out groan.

Had his shots been effective? Or was Morton trying to trick him? He cocked the Colt and cautiously stepped forward, sliding from tree to tree, until he spied an odd shape ahead. A man was seated at the base of a forest giant, leaning on the bole. He distinguished the ashen hue of a face and heard more bitter laughter.

"You're good, Trailsman. Never saw anyone move so damn fast."

Fargo wasn't about to show himself and be mowed down in a hail of lead. He aimed at Morton's chest and said, "Stand up and hold your hands out where I can see them."

The gunman snorted. "My standing days are over, thanks to you." He coughed violently and gasped for breath before adding, "And I can't lift my arms more than a couple of inches."

Fargo still wasn't taking any chances. He moved closer, stepping from tree to tree, until he was two yards from the outlaw. The dull glint of metal drew his eyes to the grass in front of Morton where the outlaw's pistols had fallen. Both of Morton's hands were empty, hanging slack at his side.

"Afraid, Trailsman?" Morton said and chuckled. "Why don't you come over here so I can bite your legs off?"

Holding the Colt steady, Fargo moved up to the gunman. There were large dark stains on the front of Morton's shirt and blood trickling from the corner of the man's mouth. "You picked the wrong line of work," he said.

"I did all right for myself. Never went hungry and always had a little money in my pocket. That's more than you can say about some of those poor honest bastards who work like slaves for a living."

Fargo slowly lowered the .44. "How far off is Killian?"

"Go to hell."

"It doesn't matter if you tell me. I'll find him soon anyway."

Morton coughed once more, then rasped, "I hope you do. He's more than a match for you. I only wish I could be there to see him pound you to a pulp."

"You have the horse before the cart," Fargo said and surveyed the pines to be certain they were alone. "Your boss won't leave this valley alive."

"Big talk, mister. But no one has clipped Ben's wings yet and you're not about to either."

Squatting so he could see Morton's face better, Fargo rested his elbows on his knees. Here was a man who had lived a life of lawlessness, greed, and mayhem. Trying to appeal to Morton's better nature, provided he even had one, would be a waste of time. But he had to try. He'd thought of something he'd overlooked. "Tell me about the children."

"What children?"

"The ones belonging to the settlers Killian had killed. I was told some of them were given to Indians. Which tribe are they living with? The Bannocks?"

"You'll never find those brats," Morton answered, smirking.

"They're kids, Morton. Innocent kids who never hurt

anyone. If I can find them I can return them to their kin. Tell me which tribe is involved?"

"Never."

Sighing, Fargo rose. If he could learn where the children were being held he'd alert the army and let the government take it from there since he wasn't about to go up against an entire tribe alone. "I should have expected this from a worthless worm like you. You don't give a damn if those children live or die."

"You're right. I don't," Morton replied.

"They deserve to be raised by relatives," Fargo commented.

"What's wrong with being reared by Injuns?" Morton retorted. "The few who we traded off will be treated decent and eat regular. You can't ask for more in this life."

"The few?" Fargo repeated. "You mean Killian murdered the rest?"

Morton grinned up at him. "What do you think, Trailsman?" He broke into a fit of convulsive coughing, his whole body shaking, blood seeping from both corners of his mouth. His eyelids fluttered and he breathed raggedly, then abruptly jerked his head skyward and exclaimed, "I'll be damned!" With that he breathed his last and slumped over, sliding to the bottom of the tree trunk. His blank eyes were fixed on Fargo's boots.

"Someone should have killed you long ago," Fargo said, a fitting epitaph, and reloaded the Colt. He hiked to the far side of the pines where he found open ground several acres in circumference and in the very center, arranged in a line with their back ends toward him, were the three Conestoga wagons. The teams had been unhitched and were grazing or resting nearby. There was no trace of a fire nor any hint of movement other than among the horses.

Where was Ben Killian? Fargo wondered. Hiding close by and waiting for him to go near the wagons so he could be easily picked off? He wasn't about to give the butcher the satisfaction. Kneeling on the carpet of brown needles under the ponderosas, he watched the wagons and bided his time. Eventually Killian would give himself away.

The seconds became minutes, the minutes became an hour. All of the horses were resting. Fargo was tempted to try and crawl to the wagons but the lack of ground cover deterred him. There were no boulders and few bushes, and the grass was too short to conceal a grown man. He'd be even easier to spot than he had been when sneaking up on the trees sheltering Morton. So he simply waited as the night waned, disliking the delay in getting back to Nellie Lee but resigned to making the best of a bad situation.

A rosy crown adorned the eastern horizon when Fargo roused his weary, sore body and stood. The wagons and field were enveloped by a gray halo. More details were visible. He studied the wagons carefully but saw no one. However he was mystified to find some of the contents of the second wagon had been tossed out and scattered all over the ground. There were tools and books and clothes lying in profusion.

Why? What had been in that wagon Killian wanted so badly? And where was Killian now? He could clearly see under the prairie schooners, and no one was hiding there. The field offered no places of concealment. Either Killian was off in one of the stands of trees with a rifle or he had fled rather than fight.

Fargo moved along the tree line, deliberately exposing himself as he dashed from trunk to trunk, trying to draw Killian's fire, but he covered twenty yards without drawing so much as a fly. Halting behind a pine, he surveyed the valley. The only living thing he saw was an owl winging its way to its daytime roost.

Slowly the sky brightened. Both the field and the wagons were bathed in sunlight. Ground squirrels came out of their burrows to greet the dawn and scampered about in energetic abandon.

Fargo watched with interest as a pair of the rodents frolicked around and under the wagons. They displayed not the slightest fear. It was as plain as the nose on his face that the wagons had been abandoned and Ben Killian was gone. As a final test he abruptly walked into the open, the Colt out and the hammer cocked.

Nothing happened.

He jogged toward the wagons, covering them in case he was wrong. The ground squirrels scattered in a panic, venting their shrill whistles and flicking their tails in anger at the intrusion. In the distance a hawk soared.

The horses regarded him indifferently as they went about munching on the dew-laden grass. A tranquil scene if ever there was one.

Fargo halted at the rear of the third wagon. He gripped the top of the tailgate, braced his boot on a wheel, and raised up to peer within. The collection of stolen articles was astounding. In the corner was a stove. In the middle sat a heavy plow. There were sacks of flour, pots and pans, a rocking chair, and even a grandfather clock. He saw a vase and a tea kettle and a mirror. In California the contents of this one wagon would bring in thousands of dollars.

Jumping down, he walked to the second wagon, stepping over the objects scattered all over the ground. He figured Killian must have been in a hurry to leave and gazed at the end of the valley, seeking evidence of another way out. At the tailgate he climbed up, his left hand grasping the top crosspiece. Inside was a shambles. All the merchandise had been thrown around and now lay piled in jumbled heaps. Just below him was a large mound of blankets of all colors and different sizes. He idly stared at them and began to lower himself off the wagon when from out of the depths of the mound swept an enormous callused fist that caught him flush on the jaw and sent him flying. Dazed by the surprise assault, he was dimly aware of crashing onto his back. He heard heavy footsteps and the Colt was torn from his grasp. Then his vision cleared and he found himself looking up into the leering face of Ben Killian.

"Got you, you son of a bitch! I knew you'd fall for the bait."

Fargo put his hands flat on the grass and sat up. Killian made no move to stop him. He felt supremely stupid for having been outfoxed so handily. If he had been using his head he would have made a complete circuit of the parked wagons to determine if there were hoof prints leading away from them. His jaw ached like hell, and it was all he could do to speak. "You're not as dumb as I figured," he remarked.

Ben Killian's right boot flicked out, smacking Fargo in the chest and knocking him flat again. Killian beamed, thoroughly enjoying himself. "In a minute I'm going to shut that smart mouth of yours forever." He hurled the

Colt far into the field, then balled his great hands into fists. "I take it you took care of Richter and Morton. Too bad. They were good men, the best I had next to Curry." He paused. "What happened to him, by the way?"

Fargo held his right hand as if it were a gun and lowered his thumb onto his forefinger.

"Didn't think anyone could beat him," Killian said. He suddenly glowered and leaned forward. "All the more reason for me to make the most of this. I want you dead, mister, but I want to kill you with my bare hands. I want to feel your bones break. I want to see you squirm and beg for mercy." He uttered a laugh that sounded more like the bark of a rabid dog. "Why do you think I went to all this trouble on your account?"

"You've found religion?" Fargo quipped, keenly aware he was in for the fight of his life. Ben Killian was a powerhouse, as formidable an enemy as he had ever faced. The man's muscles stood out in cords on his neck and it was a safe guess his shoulders and arms were like iron bands.

"Never learn, do you?" Killian countered. He backed up several feet and lifted his fists as a boxer would do. "On your feet, idiot. And do me a favor. Try to make this interesting. Nine times out of ten I kill a man in the first two minutes."

"I'll do my best," Fargo said, starting to rise, knowing Killian expected him to stand upright before they clashed. But another tactic he had learned from the Indians came to mind, namely to always do the unexpected. Any man who was predictable in battle seldom lasted long. So, as he uncoiled, he thrust his arms on the ground and swung his legs in a vicious circle, slamming them into Killian's shins.

The hulking brute's eyes widened in amazement as he toppled forward. He landed on his hands and knees, then surged upright, his features livid.

Fargo stood near the wagon. He deliberately smiled and said as if bored, "I don't see why you have the reputation you do. You're nothing but a lumbering ox who doesn't have the brains God gave a turnip."

Killian roared like a grizzly and recklessly charged, his arms outspread to catch the Trailsman in a bear hug from which there would be no escape, an embrace that would crush Fargo's ribs as if they were twigs and snap his spine as if it was a dry limb. Always before in such fits of rage he had overpowered and slain his foes before he quite knew what he was doing, driven temporarily over the brink by his berserk fury. This time would be no different.

Fargo seemed to have grown roots. But although he was motionless, his mind raced as he gauged the distance between them, and when Killian's hands were within inches of his broad shoulders he ducked and darted to the right. At the same time he kicked out with his left leg. He felt Killian trip over his ankle and heard a crunch as the gang leader's forehead smashed into the Conestoga. Back-pedaling a half-dozen feet to give himself room to move, he crouched and awaited the next attack.

"Damn you!" Killian snarled, spinning and pressing a hand to the bloody gash in his brow.

"There's more where that came from," Fargo said, pleased at the ease with which he could spark Killian's anger. An angry man was a careless man, and a careless man was soon a dead one.

Killian took a lunging stride, then checked himself, his eyes narrowing in crafty insight. "Clever," he said. "Real clever. But it won't work twice." He moved forward warily, his ponderous fists clenched tight.

Fargo slowly backed up. Trading blows would be pointless. Killian wasn't the type to go down quickly and an extended fight would be in Killian's favor. The lack of rest and the crease in his forehead were bound to take their toll early on, giving the butcher an easy victory. If he was to have any hope of surviving, he must rely on his wits instead of his strength.

"Stand and fight, you yellowbelly!" Killian hissed, advancing steadily.

"You're forgetting something, Ben," Fargo said. He stopped and turned so that his left side was to the butcher.

"What might that be?" Killian responded, taking another measured pace.

"My knife," Fargo said and sank down as if grabbing for the Arkansas toothpick, his right hand dropping to the top of his boot.

Killian, forgetting himself, sprang in a diving tackle while bellowing, "No you don't!"

In a sense Killian was right. Fargo had no intention of drawing the blade. It was a ploy, a ruse that worked perfectly, for as Killian leaped with outstretched arms Skye whirled and drove his right fist up and in, straight into Killian's neck. The blow rocked Killian in midair and he fell, gurgling in acute torment and clutching at his smashed throat. Skye moved in, and when Killian, sputtering and snorting, went to rise, he landed not one but two punches to the side of Killian's neck that flattened the man at his feet.

"No!" Killian rasped in a hoarse whisper. "Not like this!" Still game, he again tried to stand.

Skye Fargo pivoted and walked out to the area where his Colt had been tossed. He searched in the grass, glancing at Killian now and again. The butcher got to his knees, then straightened on wobbly legs and staggered toward the wagon. Fargo found the revolver just as Killian reached the back of the Conestoga. He turned as Killian reached into a corner and pulled out a rifle. And he squeezed off his first shot as Killian tried to level his weapon. Killian tottered, grimacing, his arms sagging, then attempted to lift the rifle once more. This time Fargo fired three times, and on the third shot Ben Killian pitched onto his face, never to rise again.

Skye Fargo lowered the Colt. At last it was over. He turned and headed up the valley to retrieve the Ovaro. Once in the saddle he would round up the stock and return to Nellie Lee. Then there would be a ride of several days to the Oregon Trail, a ride that promised pleasant company in the daytime, and nights of fiery passion.

He could live with it.

LOOKING FORWARD!

**The following is the opening
section from the next novel in the exciting
Trailsman series from Signet:**

THE TRAILSMAN #129
THE SILVER MARIA

---

*1860, New Mexico Territory,
a simmering desert
where men will stake their lives,
betray their friends and sell their souls
to find the lost legend of the Silver Maria . . .*

"Tell me where it is. Now."

He heard the words through the roaring in his ears, and he willed the muscles of his tired neck to shake his head.

"Never," he heard himself say, as if from a distance. The warm blood was dripping down his neck. He felt the searing pain where his ears had been torn and sliced from his head. Soon it wouldn't matter. The man had already killed Barney and thrown his body into the pit. Soon he would kill him too. How long? Time had no meaning here under the blazing sun, his blood running down his neck. But he would bear any pain.

He looked up into the face of the man. He had never trusted him. How could he have been so stupid not to see what was coming? And where were the others? The others he had trusted and led for many years? The man had ordered them to tie him spread-eagle to a boulder. Then they left, not looking back at him. Not wanting to know what would happen.

"Then I will get the information out of Antonia," the man hissed. "Yes, that will be a pleasure."

He felt the breath leave his body and pain, pain he could not bear, clutched his chest.

"Antonia knows nothing," he said. *"Nada."*

The man struck his face with all his force, and he felt his head bounce painfully against the boulder.

"Don't speak that Spanish shit to me! Tell me. Where is the Silver Maria?"

He hesitated as the man drew his knife and took a step forward. He looked up into the man's face and saw there the curse that had killed men and made men kill other men for over three hundred years. He saw lust for blood, for silver, in the other man's face. And he smiled. He couldn't help himself. A tight smile, a grimace of pain, of recognition.

The man screamed with rage and lunged forward, knife upraised, grasping his hair with one hand. He closed his eyes tight, straining against the ropes and felt the excruciating heat of the knife piercing his eyelid, entering his eye, twisting, rough-cutting his eye out of the socket. Throbbing blackness welled up around him and he heard from a distance, "Tell me. Where. Now. Or Antonia dies. Or worse."

The words were wrenched out of him and he tasted his blood in his mouth. "Mission . . . Ascension. Padre . . . Ernesto." He felt the void of despair after the words were spoken. "Just . . . leave . . . Antonia . . . alone."

"She's a pretty little snot," the man said, tightening the grip on his scalp. "Too pretty to be left alone."

Then, far away, he felt the man grasp his scalp again. More pain, but duller, his other eye cut out, the heat pouring down his face and an odd coolness on his forehead, a lightness, like floating. Then a fumbling, his arms and legs being cut free of the ropes and falling, landing on something soft. Barney, he thought. His loyal friend. And with the last of his remaining strength, he contracted his muscles, embracing the man who lay under him at the bottom of the sand pit. He felt Barney stir.

He realized he would bleed to death, here at the bottom of this pit in the desert heat, his eyes cut out of their sockets, his ears sliced off. Send Antonia help, he said in his mind. But who could help her when the curse of the Silver Maria corrupted all men? And suddenly the picture of a tall, silent man riding alone came into his mind. Maybe there was a hope. Then, above, he heard the click of a hammer. Gunfire. And nothing.

Fargo was a silent shadow, a slowly moving blacker blackness in the night as he slid silently along the side of the cabin, careful that his boots not crackle the dry gravel and that he not brush against the creaky board wall. He paused and listened. His acute hearing picked up no sounds from inside the flimsy shack. All was still.

He waited, muscles tensed, his Colt revolver glinting faintly in the pale starlight. Far off, he heard the low whistle of a screech owl and the nearer rustle of night wind over the low sage. As he rounded the corner of the building the moonlight struck him. He glanced up at the new moon hanging newly risen above the horizon against the pale starlit sky. It was nearly midnight. Where the hell was she?

Fargo edged closer to the cabin door, a tall, muscular man, wary, coiled as tightly as a spring, his face in shadow. Then he heard it. Inside. The barest dry rustle. A slight scurrying, the whisper of a movement. He tensed and moved to the door.

With a swift motion he kicked open the door and jumped aside. There was silence inside. He regarded the gaping black doorway.

"Antonia?" he said to the darkness. No answer.

He removed his hat and tossed it across the threshold. It fell inside onto the floor.

Fargo relaxed and smiled to himself. Nothing in there with a gun, he decided. He pulled the tinder box from his pocket and struck a light, holding the flame in front of him as he ducked his head into the shack and leaned down to retrieve his hat. The light lasted long enough for him to see a rusted iron bedstead, a table, and several broken chairs. A movement, a sideways scrambling on the floor, caught his eye as the light flickered and failed. He heard the dry rustle again. He backed out and pulled the door shut behind him. Scorpions, he thought. And he reminded himself to shake out his boots before putting them on in the morning.

Skye Fargo slowly scanned the terrain in front of the shack, noting the arrangement of rocks and sage. He walked quietly to a tall outcropping nearby, and climbed up several feet, bracing himself in a narrow cleft, hidden in shadow. He looked down over the solitary cabin and the trail which led to it in the dim moonlight. To the west, he saw the stark rock walls and the opening to Loyal Gulch. That was the landmark. The message said to meet her at the cabin at the mouth of Loyal Gulch. At midnight. Now where was she?

A few minutes later, Fargo heard his pinto nicker. The Ovaro, tethered out of sight in the sage, smelled something approaching. The nicker was a warning, but the pinto would not make a noise if anything strange was within earshot. Hoofbeats sounded, coming fast. Fargo cocked the Colt and waited.

On the trail he saw a lone horseman, riding hellbent, a flicker of movement on the dark sage plain. The rider galloped up the trail and pulled up short before the cabin, swinging down to dismount with a swirl of riding cape.

"Skye?"

Fargo relaxed at the sound of her voice, but did not move. He watched as she looked about nervously. She tethered the horse to the hitching post by the door of the shack.

"Skye?" she called again. Louder this time. He heard a trace of nervousness in her voice.

"*Mierda!*" she cursed in Spanish, stamping her foot impatiently. Fargo smiled to himself and watched as she paced back and forth a few times. And he listened. He listened to the silence of the trail behind her. Was she being followed? But the night stayed quiet.

Fifteen minutes passed while she paced before the cabin, patting the neck of her horse from time to time. The message from her said her life was in danger. That usually meant somebody was hard on your heels. If somebody was following her, they weren't close behind. It was time to let her know he was here.

"Antonia," he said and saw her jump. She took a stumbling step toward her horse, as if to mount. "I'm here. It's Skye Fargo." At the sound of his name she turned and peered into the darkness toward the rock outcropping.

"Skye? *Mi Dios*! Why didn't you answer me? Where are you?"

He was beside her in a moment.

"Antonia," he said as he hugged her close, noticing her soft, yielding curves under his hands. "I wanted to be sure you weren't being followed. Well, well. Antonia Delgado. It's been many, many years." He held her at arm's length. "My, how you've grown."

He had last seen her as a young girl with blazing black eyes, gawky and shy as a newborn fawn. But now before him stood a full-blown woman, her ebony hair streaming long behind her in the night wind. The riding cape and wide skirt hid the curves he had embraced. He took her chin in his hand and turned her face toward the pale moonlight. It was a beautiful face: the jet eyebrows arched and glistening above two eyes so fiery black that they glittered even in the near darkness. Her eyes hadn't changed. Her full lips smiled.

"Skye Fargo," she said in a low, rich voice. "Thank you for coming to help me. You are a true friend . . ."

"That's me," he said.

"And a friend of my father's." He heard her voice catch on the last word.

"Yes," Fargo answered. "Yes. Friend of your father's. Rest his soul. And Julio Delgado was a friend to me. When I needed him once, he saved my life."

"Well, now I need you," she said.

"Come with me," Skye said. He took Antonia by the hand and helped her up to his perch in the cleft in the rock. "From here we can watch the road behind you. Just to be sure. Your message said your life's in danger. I don't want anybody jumping us while you tell me what's up."

She settled herself between two rocks, and Fargo's

lake-blue eyes quickly scanned the nubby sage plain. No movement.

"What's going on?" he asked, directing his full attention to Antonia.

"I-I don't know," she said.

"You told me Julio was killed."

"Sí. Sí." She spat the words, bitter words, and Fargo saw tears of sorrow and rage glisten in her dark eyes. She held up her hand, as much to halt him from answering as to stop her tears. "Crying will not bring him back," she said. "My father was a hero. He truly lived every moment of his life, holding nothing back. I will not cry. It does him dishonor." Fargo watched as she bit her lower lip and regained control.

Watching her, he thought of Colonel Julio Delgado as he had last seen him years ago, waving good-bye, sitting high on his mount in his U.S. Army uniform. Delgado had been a legendary fighter in the war with Mexico and had been rewarded with the command post at Fort Managa.

The command hadn't been an easy one. Fort Managa was a lonely outpost, Fargo remembered. After the war there had been many years of constant trouble with Mexican raids across the border. And recently the Apache had been tricked by unscrupulous settlers and treaties, and had become even more ferocious.

But Colonel Julio Delgado had been equal to all this and more. In Julio's veins ran the mixed blood of Spanish nobility, Mexican grit, Indian cunning, and white ambition. He had been a man that other men would follow, tireless, selfless, brave. A man who rode in front of his men into battle. A man who never asked his men to do what he would not.

Julio Delgado had saved his life once, risking his own to free him from the Apache. It had been a long time ago. And now Delgado was dead, his lovely daughter left alone. Fargo felt an old, familiar cold rage kindle in his chest. Delgado's was a murder that would not go unpunished.

"Tell me how it happened," Fargo said.

CANYON O'GRADY RIDES ON